Bernadette Kane

Bernadette Kane is from Glasgow, Scotland, where she lives. She spends her time writing and painting. Her love for the Loch on her doorstep, Loch Lomond, regularly draws her outdoors for wild camps and swims. The incredible scenery of her native Scotland is a continuous source of inspiration, both for her writing and her landscape paintings. She studied Theology and Literature at St. Andrews University, and was awarded their top prize for Excellence in Literature, the Lawson Memorial Prize.

Dear Susan,
Hope you love this!
Bernadette
xxx
January 2022

ACKNOWLEDGEMENTS

Heartfelt thanks to my loyal band of readers, who kept me going with the writing of *Dancing with India, Finding Shanthi,* during the long lockdown. They are, in no particular order, Anita Nanjappa, expert in all things India, Helen Kane, Helen MacDonald, Elizabeth Anne Conetta, and James Kane.

Thank you!

Note: This is a novel and a work of fiction and, apart from the public figures mentioned, all characters are fictional. Any resemblance to actual people, living or dead, is coincidental.

Cover painting: "Dawn", by Bernadette Kane.

DANCING WITH INDIA

Finding Shanthi

Bernadette Kane

For Danny, my brother.

Prologue

Covid-19 is well into its second year when Marney McDonagh, finding herself isolated and alone during the endless lockdown, hits on an idea to help save her sanity. She's going to start an online writing group. And she already knows what she wants to write.

At the start of the pandemic, she remembered Daniel Defoe's old classic novel, A Journal of the Plague Year. That book had been written three hundred years before, way back in 1722, and Defoe had claimed it to be his own daily diary. He had kept a record, he said, of his experiences during the devastating Bubonic Plague of 1665, and his Journal was that record.

This Journal had been something of a sham though, as Marney remembered from her student days at Glasgow University. She recalled that Defoe had only been five years old at the time of the Great Plague, and that he had created his journal by reading other people's accounts of it, and then presenting them as his own first-hand experiences.

Marney decides though, that she will keep a true, authentic record of one person's life, her own, as well as track the worldwide battle against the virus. It would help her pass the time, she thought, and who knew, one day it might just provide an accurate account of these crazy days.

But when she sees the billowing clouds of smoke rising up from the makeshift crematoria springing up all over Delhi as the people of India become overwhelmed by the numbers of Covid dead, Marney finds herself plunged into a deep reminiscence of how her many years spent in that country all began.

From a Covid lockdown in Glasgow, Marney's journal dives back fifteen years, to her arrival at Shanthi Ashram. Her stories of ashram life buzz with all the fire-cracking colour and passion of the Indian South, and the exotic band of characters whom she meets, with their deep joys, passionate intrigues and utter horrors, give her a glimpse into a new and fascinating world.

As Marney listens to the daily talks by Brother Joseph, the ashram's Spiritual Teacher, and spends long afternoons with the Sadhu who lives in the forest, her knowledge and understanding of Indian spirituality grow, forcing her to look more deeply than ever before into what it means to be human.

***

14th March 2021

Waiting for Geraldine and Julie to arrive. This is our first Zoom Writing Club meeting, and I'm excited at the prospect of journaling again. Although I'm forever telling everyone else that they should be writing, I never actually do it myself. It's been ages since I've put pen to paper, so to speak, even though I know, intimately, how hugely therapeutic it is, how it can, like no other exercise, work at shifting the boulders and rubble which stifle and block the psyche.

I managed to persuade them both, as we chatted through our masks on our daily walks, that this interminable lockdown was the ideal time to start a new project, a creative one, and that writing was the very best way to get those pent-up feelings outside of you, leaving you much more free on the inside.

It's as if the process of writing is a way of emptying yourself out, I said, or at least emptying out whatever it is that's clogging up your life, your spirit, your sense of freedom.

For some reason, I continued, we seem to want to hold onto our baggage, as if we're afraid of losing it, but what I've found is that because you're actually recording it all in writing, you don't feel that you're losing it, or even letting it go, because in fact you're capturing it on paper.

It really works, I said. On the one hand you're free because you've expressed it, and on the other hand, you've still got it and you can look at it whenever you want. But you'll be looking at it on your own terms, and from a safe distance.

I spoke about it passionately, as one who had already experienced the exciting adventure of allowing yourself free rein on a page and reaped some of its benefits, and at last they agreed. They both confessed that they'd felt drawn to writing for a while – Geraldine had even taken to browsing through the journaling notebooks in gift shops and had bought herself three deluxe ones so far, ones covered in pretty pink sparkles and bound with blue ribbon.

But they didn't know how to start, and wanted our first Zoom session to be just a get-together over coffee and a chat about the process of writing, and most importantly, *what* to write. And so we agreed to meet up in the coming week and do just that.

I already know what I want to do in my own writing project, and my mission is a simple one – to make a written record of life during this crazy time of Covid. I also want to stay semi-sane during this mind-blowing and endless lockdown. Spending hours on end painting has always been the best therapy, stepping out of the mind and becoming lost in the slap and splash of paint on canvas, but now something else is needed to fill the endless hours of isolation. And writing a journal during these plague years is it!

21st March 2021

Met my writing buddy Geraldine again on this morning's walk. Her big, daft dog Pluto was barking away like crazy, just like Jade used to when she wasn't the centre of attention – the walk was her time, and she would not be ignored. I picked Pluto up and squeezed her hard under my arm. She seemed to like that – the squeeze, and the attention, and the barking stopped.

We chatted excitedly about our new online group, recapping on the main points from our recent meeting. We were both thrilled to be writing, and writing in good company, sharing the fruits of our pens and getting feedback from each other. She had been having a real battle with her mental health these past few months, swinging between depression and elation, and the bipolar disorder she had struggled with since adolescence had been exacerbated by the pandemic. She was loving the writing project, and finding great release through giving voice to all that had been happening within her during lockdown.

Writing it all down, she said, transforming it into something beautiful, is like opening a safety valve.

She had plunged immediately into poetry – short, vivid pieces filled with anguish and joy and energetic imagery from the natural world – tempest tossed seas, dandelion seed heads, blown apart by the wind into a million scattering pieces, daisy-chains, threaded with care then broken and trampled underfoot, the Spring sap rising up, with great force, to burst open the tender buds of May, their blossoms dancing in the sunshine.

Each poem seemed to contain a similar dynamic – something fragile and beautiful, natural, being broken and scattered, and then the resolution, when all the fragmented pieces came together again, and cohered. They were beautiful poems, reflecting Geraldine herself, with all her fragility, and all her strength.

As we walked along the banks of the Clyde Canal, throwing the ball for Pluto, we eventually lapsed back into moaning and groaning about lockdown. Again. An increasingly frequent topic of conversation. We'd had over a year of it by now, with only a short break over autumn, when the virus became briefly quiescent. During that break, we had all rushed around like mad things, meeting up for coffees, and lunches, and dinners, and walks. But then the numbers had begun to soar, and we found ourselves back at home, alone, and in solitary confinement.

The things we had once taken for granted – walking in the park with a friend, coffee and cream topped walnut cake in the Botanicals Tearoom, lunch with Molly at Epicures, visits to my brother Don and sister-in-law Clare, to eat more cake and bond with their new Dalmatian rescue Spotty, abandoned after his years as a stud were over; all these things, all these little things, all these unremarkable things, had ended abruptly, and for the last year we had been confined to barracks, allowed outside only for shopping, exercise or to seek medical help.

We had, like half the nation, become fat slobs, lolling about on couches, stuffing our faces and watching Netflix, pulling ourselves up off the couch only to hobble to the fridge, and back again.

Geraldine and I first met on the banks of the Canal around four years ago. I had been bug-eyed with stress at the time, and was walking briskly along the Canal path, trying to calm down. The man I'd hired to manage my apartment renovation, to relieve me of the stress of it, had just been begun extorting large sums of money. Five thousand pounds more he wanted, he said, because someone he trusted told him that he should have charged much more in the first place.

His threatening and increasingly desperate emails were terrifying. I was alone in the house with no-one close by. He knew where I lived. He'd been here. I paid him two and half thousand pounds by bank transfer and took some tranquillisers to stop the shaking. Then I went for a walk and met Geraldine and Pluto. When she saw me coming towards her, Geraldine just stopped and looked... Her eyes were soft and sensitive, and she seemed to know that I was in a state.

Are you okay? she asked.

No, I blurted out, and it didn't seem to matter that I didn't know her, or that I had never met her before. I just blurted out the whole sorry tale.

22nd March 2021

Saw a big strong Magpie when I got up this morning, through my bleary waking eyes, doing battle in the back garden hedging. A single magpie - sorrow, trouble ahead ... trouble now for whatever poor creature was being repeatedly stabbed and pummeled by that huge beak. I was just about to go outside on a rescue mission, save the poor thing, shoo away the aggressive bringer of bad news, but then, as the pie flew off, beakful of twig and branch, the penny dropped.

Spring had finally arrived.

After our first fateful meeting on the Canal banks four years ago, I didn't see Geraldine again until last month, this time on the Great Western Road. I was talking to a dog walker, feeding love-heart shaped chicken treats to her dog, when Geraldine appeared, bright and cheerful, Pluto in tow. She knew the woman whose dog I had accosted but didn't know me, nor I her, until we began chatting to each other.

Geraldine was first to recognise me, and immediately recalled our last meeting. So much had happened for me in the intervening years that I could barely recall the horror of being threatened and extorted. Nor did I want to recall it, it had been so devastating, but I remembered Geraldine, and my bug-eyed confession of distress by the Canal.

I wonder if she thinks I'm mad I thought, quickly straightening up and pulling myself together, trying to appear not just normal, but a very much together woman of substance. The meeting was unnerving though, and the memories of that time did come rushing back.

Inside the house again, after a brandy to calm me, the flow of distressing memory slowed down, and the recollections of that time became clearer.

The episode of threat and extortion by Henry had been the last in a series of shocks which stretched back deep into my mother's dying years. Those long last years were so dreadful for us both, and so filled with stress, and anxiety, and pain. It was ghastly watching her, this strong, brilliant woman who loved life so passionately, dying slowly as the pulmonary fibrosis, caused by the renal failure pills, began claiming more and more of her lungs, and every day became a struggle just to keep breathing, just to stay alive.

There had been so many crises, so many emergency hospital admissions, so many near death experiences, that when she did finally pass away, it still came as a terrible shock.

It was a full two years after that, that a return to something like normal life began again, and it began in the form of the project to renovate my two bedroomed apartment in the West End, and get it ready for the market.

It had been bought twenty-four years previously, just after I started teaching. But ten years later, when increasingly frequent bouts of anxiety and depression had sent me running off to India for respite, it was rented out through an agency. The rent money was initially intended to fund a six month' stay at Shanthi ashram, beside the tiny village of Paripalli in South India. What I didn't know back then, was that India would burst my heart wide open and enter my bloodstream forever after.

As the twists and turns of life unfolded from that trip, becoming split between India and Drumknock, it was this money which kept things ticking over. I never did return to live in the apartment again, and just trusted that the letting agency was doing its job of maintaining the place and ensuring that the tenants were keeping it in good nick.

But they didn't. They simply collected the rent, took their fifteen percent, and let the tenants run amuck. Fifteen years later, the place had descended into a complete and filthy mess.

What a massive job of work it was – new plumbing, electrical rewiring, new kitchen and bathroom, new fireplace, new windows, new floors, old walls re-plastered – the place needed to be completely ripped out from the inside and rebuilt.

Amongst all the adverts for refurbishment experts on the internet, good old Henry and his Sterling Renovations business stood out. After a call to his mobile, an interview for the following day was arranged.

He arrived bang on time, laden with swatches of wallpaper and colour charts and design ideas, and two fresh coffees from Starbucks. A nice touch. He was good looking, smooth talking, and suave, with his manicured blonde locks, sparkling brown eyes and lean muscular body. He went over his impressive credentials in detail, proudly showing all the glowing reports from satisfied clients. He got the job on the spot.

Sipping our coffees, we went over the works required, and the extent of his role as Project Manager. His remit and fees were agreed, and Henry went home to draw up the contract. The next day we signed it and, as per the remit, he was paid fifty percent up front, with the remaining fifty percent to be paid upon completion of the project.

The job took three hectic months to complete, and at the end of that time Henry received the balance of his bill, together with the promise of an additional ten percent bonus when the apartment was sold. We were both thrilled with the works, and stood together in the apartment, admiring its complete transformation from a filthy dump of a place into a sparkling new luxury apartment.

Around a week later Henry was back in touch again. The ten percent bonus, he said, wasn't enough. He wanted more. Now. Immediately. Five thousand pounds more. I refused. And then the threats began. He knew that he'd been hired because I couldn't handle stress, and he worked on that knowledge, eventually triggering me into a state of panic. I sent him the two and half thousand pounds by bank transfer and tried to relax.

He wrote again, giving me two weeks to come up with the rest of the money.

By now I was truly freaking out, and relieved that my lawyer was also a good friend. It was easy to tell Eileen the story. She was horrified. He shouldn't have been paid anything more at all, she said, and rang off with the instruction to tell him that he should direct all further correspondence to her.

After that, Henry began threatening her, nicely of course, and through the façade of politesse which he had mastered, to take me to Court.

Eileen was more than a match for him though, and she kept him at arm's length during the six weeks of his relentless attempts to get another two and a half thousand pounds, despite the fact that he was completely in the wrong, and that all the paperwork showed this. She just kept calling his bluff and reminding him that, when we met in Court, she would be suing him for the return of the money which he had extorted.

Eventually he gave up.

But it was shattering, and all plans to buy another place to renovate and resell died the death. The stress of dealing with people like Henry just wasn't an option.

But all that had been years ago, and forgotten about, until Geraldine appeared, and it all came flooding back.

23rd March 2021

Today is the first anniversary of Britain's first move into lockdown, and the news is full of it – pictures of Boris Johnson, much plumper back then, before his brush with death at the hands of the virus, and hair more unruly, addressing the nation in his plummy accent and *Good Old Days* vocabulary, trying to appear like a statesman, but all the while looking like the caricature of a naughty public schoolboy, cap askew and tie off to one side, shirt-tails hanging out, flying in the wind.... The statistics, the cases, the hospitalisations, the deaths; the elderly care home scandal; teary-eyed citizens remembering their lost loved ones; care workers applauded at eight o'clock each evening, as they became increasingly haggard and exhausted and grief stricken, but still battling against the virus, and against the lack of PPE, and equipment, and medicines, and staff.

A dreadful time it was, the start of the first wave.

I should have been in India when Covid began, way up in the blue mountains of the South, in a little town called Kamun - a beautiful place, which the British had taken over during the days of the Raj to set up their summer headquarters. It was just too hot for their fair skins in Madras, and so when Ian MacGregor, one of their number, had spotted these high hills way off in the distance and set out to explore them, it didn't take long for them all to relocate there and commence their transformation of these once pristine tribal lands and untouched nature into a miniature version of a town in Sussex.

It was during my second long trip to India that I first went to Kamun, sent there by a Sadhu who told me to seek out an old English woman who had been living in these hills for many years. The Sadhu gave me her name and location, promising that she could help fulfil what had become my mission – to assist in the rescue of baby girls from infanticide, something I had learned of at Shanthi Ashram, and which I hoped to help alleviate.

My stay in Kamun had barely begun when Auntie Chat, a neighbour, brought a beautiful, dark-eyed and mysterious young woman into my room. She was relocating to Kamun, Auntie Chat said, and was looking for a place to stay. It wasn't until sometime later that Annika told me her story, along with the hair-raising reasons that she had fled into the hills.

We soon became friends, and in the next few years we shared what was my second great adventure in India together. It was through Annika, with her acute sharpness of mind and keen observation, that the roots of what had ailed me throughout life were eventually laid bare, and the help needed to bring about a kind of rebirth was found.

We're still friends, and my usual winter habit is to go to Kamun, staying close to her little house, Blue Diamond. The months spent there, painting in the gardens outside the rooms at Mount Hermon Lodge, trekking the hills, which turned a brilliant shade of blue every twelve years when the Kurinji flowers bloomed, were the best of winter sunshine.

Annika is a remarkable woman, a uniquely creative one. Her rare kind of creativity is one which is always reaching out to others, either to help ease their suffering, or to bring beauty and joy into their lives.

On my last trip, the year before Covid came rolling in, I worked beside her as she created a new art gallery in town, a gallery which was being made from a disused public toilet. It was such a novel idea, rescuing a putrid and stinking eyesore slap-bang in the middle of town, and turning it into something beautiful. Within months, the smelly, flooded, sewage filled toilet had been transformed into a sparkling new art space, and, with a nod to its previous function, it was dubbed, Gallery OneTwo.

But a bout of ill health last winter meant that I couldn't have managed that journey all the way up to Kamun - the two long flights, and then the long bumpy jeep ride up into the mountains.

Instead, my cousin Nuala in Puerto Pollensa found me a place to stay, close to her on the island, for the whole of the winter, and so I gladly accepted the offer.

It was a fab place, about a fifteen minutes' walk from the beach and it had a conservatory which doubled as a light-filled, airy studio. Winter there was warm and bright, and though it wasn't the incredible India, it did have sunshine, beautiful views, sandy beaches and turquoise seas, as well as a lively expat community. My paintings were attracting attention and sales beginning to flow in to such an extent that all my costs were covered, and there was a bit left over. It was a great place to be over winter, and I was loving it.

I was still in Mallorca when the virus came charging through Europe, firstly devastating communities in Northern Italy and then mainland Spain. The Spanish authorities panicked, and imposed the strictest lockdown possible – *we were not allowed out at all without documentation proving that we were on an essential journey for emergency purposes.*

It was hellish.

The streets were deserted of all but slowly moving, prowling Police cars, like sluggish blue and white beetles, patrolling the streets on the lookout for anyone who had dared to venture out beyond their own front doors. Essential shops – food and medicine stores, could open, but only two or three people were allowed in at a time, and everyone was masked, and sanitised, and Policed.

Supplies of masks and hand sanitiser quickly ran out, causing even more panic amongst some, creativity amongst others. I Googled a recipe and made gallons of sanitizer from aloe vera gel and pure alcohol, resisting the temptation to just drink it all. It worked, but it made my hands dry and rough as sandpaper. Scarves became improvised face coverings, and life limped and lurched towards a new norm.

28th March 2021

This should have been Easter Sunday. Six weeks ago, forty days to be precise, I gave up my evening brandy for Lent – the first time I've been without my nightcap for maybe ten years. It was tough at first, and I almost fell on a few occasions, but focusing on this day, forty days after Pancake Tuesday, when I could re-imbibe, kept me going.

It wasn't until Thursday that it began to dawn on me that my calculation must be off. As I reckoned it, forty days equals six weeks, give or take a couple of days, bringing the end of Lent in at the twenty-eighth of March, the day which I had been eagerly anticipated for so long. But then Janet sent a text.

Next Saturday, she wrote, is part of the Easter Triduum, and should we go ahead with our Art Club meeting?

Next Saturday, I squawked. Surely she's mistaken.

I hastily Googled Easter Sunday, 2021. Horror. Easter Sunday this year is actually on the fourth of April. How could this have happened? Had I not actually been abstemious for six weeks? Had it only been five? No. Surely not. Next, I Googled the number of days in Lent. Forty. It was definitely forty.

Then the small print - Sundays are not included!

Bloody hell! Is Sunday not a day? Did those six abstemious Sundays count for nought?

Apparently so.

The feeble excuse offered by Wikipedia is that Sundays are considered to be holy days anyway, and so are not included in the forty.

Pff.

What nonsense.

Utterly cheesed off, I thought, I'm having a brandy *now*. I've done the forty days. No-one ever said anything about forty nine days. I'd been tricked. In the kitchen cupboard, I fished out the half full brandy bottle and the cut crystal glass.

This needs a bit of a clean, I thought, surveying the glass, a bit of a polish...

Then I put it down again, and decided to wait.

Another six days to go.

29th March 2021

Got vaccinated on Thursday, Oxford Astra Zeneca, the one the European Union has put on hold because of reports of blood clotting in some patients. All nonsense, of course, say the British Government - there's no more clotting in the vaccinated group than in the general population per capita. The European Union are at it, their spokesman says, simply indulging in a post-Brexit tat-for-tat.

Is this our future, our petty partisan future? Fish suppers have gone up by eighty pence – more than a ten percent rise – because of Brexit and the endless squabble over fishing rights. Can't bear it. The whole world is squabbling, shouting, screaming, fighting, raping, stealing, lying ... the whole world, the whole beautiful, crying, dying, screaming world, in a seemingly endless agony.

But I'm glad to be vaccinated. No blood clots yet. Though who knows where the truth is. One may still appear.

Easter Sunday, 4th April 2021

Feeling sick. Two days now. Upset tummy, or rather, upset lower down in the gut, below the waist. Feels like food poisoning. Must have been the chocolate from Aldi's on Good Friday. No Easter eggs left, so I bought a packet of Maltesers, another of Minstrels and one of Revels, and then went home and scoffed the lot, in lieu of an egg. Began feeling awful a few hours later, and it's lasted until now.

This binging on chocolate has become a regular feature of lockdown, and the pounds are piling on.

My Easter celebrations began early, with a brandy at one minute past midnight on Good Friday. I would like to blame my cousin Nuala for this lapse. She, despite me imploring her not to, had wine on Good Friday.

This is *the* most fast and abstinence day of them all, I had squawked at her, but no, she said, this is the day on which he saved us, and I'll drink to that.

Easter Monday, 5th April 2021

Clare, my sister-in-law, visited this morning, bringing the sunshine of her smile and an armful of Easter gifts. She couldn't come into the house because of the restrictions, and so we just chatted outside in the front garden for a while. She had brought a beautiful posy of Spring flowers – daffodils and daisies, purple irises and lily of the valley, and the most sweet-smelling buttercup-yellow freesia.

She also brought a huge white Easter egg from Hotel Chocolat, all wrapped up in cellophane and tied with bonnie pink ribbons. Only the best. Thick white chocolate shell filled with handmade white chocolate treats. So delicious that I ate it. Oddly enough, it didn't make me feel sick. That's quality for you.

I sometimes wondered whether my brother Don and his wife Clare had anything to do with Covid, because whenever they went to China, something kind of earth shattering would happen.

The first time was when they went to Beijing to play in the Bridge World Championship – Clare was a player, and Don the Team Coach. They stayed in the somewhat ironically named Beijing Renaissance Hotel, situated right beside the Communist Party Conference

Halls, and while they were busily playing Bridge, right next door, Xi Jinping was declaring himself as something of a deity. From that moment on, the Party announced, Xi would be China's leader for his entire life, and the Constitution would be rewritten to reflect his thoughts and philosophy.

Even though they were completely absorbed in the Championship, they were aware of the tension around the place, and an incident which happened during one of their nights there seemed to sum it up.

They had been awakened at two in the morning by loud shouting from the room next door – one side of a phone conversation. They managed to ignore this, but when it happened again the next night, Don decided that he'd had enough. He began by battering his fist on the wall, to let the shouter know that he was disturbing their sleep, and when the shouting continued, he went out onto the landing and battered on the door. Still no response, and still the shouting continued.

He returned to the room and telephoned Reception to complain. The young woman Receptionist quickly appeared, flanked by two strapping young men, and together they managed to get the shouter out of his room and onto the landing, at which point he began kicking violently at Don and Clare's door, trying to break it down.

Eventually the staff managed to quiet the man, and when they thought he was calm, the Receptionist knocked softly on the door, asking Don and Clare to come out.

When they came out onto the landing, Don and Clare could see that the staff were afraid of the man, trying to placate him, and just as the Receptionist was timidly asking Don to apologise to the man, the man lunged forward and took a kick at him. Don, who had been a professional boxer back in the day, selected to spar with Mohammed Ali at the Kelvin Hall back in the seventies, lightly skipped backwards and to the side, so that the man, finding no target for his kick, stumbled forward, infuriated.

Don then stepped back again, into his range, at which point the man kicked out at him again, and again, Don skipped back, further infuriating the man, whose face had by now begun turning into all shades of purple.

The Receptionist hadn't noticed Don's light skips backwards, and thinking that the man had landed a blow on him, she had called the Police. Two large burly officers quickly arrived, and when they saw who the man was, they too became intimidated, asking Don and Clare to return to their room while they spoke with him.

Some minutes later, there was another knock on their door, and when they came back out onto the landing, the Reception staff and the Policemen, all of whom were clearly afraid, remonstrated with Don, telling him that the man needed an apology from him, for the sake of his honour, and begged him to do so. The Receptionist, by now in floods of tears, believing Don to have been assaulted by the man and conflicted by the irony of his having to apologise to him, crumpled with relief when Don told her that the man's kick had missed him.

It was Don's habit to spend months before each foreign trip learning something of the language, so that when he saw the nature of the situation he found himself in, he was able to say,

Ni yow woa shaw dui bu chi?

Meaning, do you wish me to apologise to him?

The startled Receptionist, taken aback, just nodded her head vigorously, and Don reached out his hand, and apologised to the man. In Chinese, of course.

They never did learn who the man was, but reckoned him to be someone of importance in the Party, and they were rewarded for their troubles by an immediate upgrade to a plush suite and the waiving of all their extraneous bills.

Their next trip to China was two years later, in September of 2019. It was for the Bridge World Championship again, but this time the venue was in Wuhan, and their hotel was just a few miles from the Wuhan Virology Laboratory. At that time, almost no-one had heard of Wuhan, but within weeks of their return, it was a household name. And when Covid began devastating the place, it was their Bridge venue which became the massive hospital which dealt with the surging cases.

Don and Clare have now vowed never to return to China.

6th April 2021

Lockdown is driving me mad. One walk per day, a bit of shopping now and then, and the occasional Zoom chat. I've seen as much of the news as I can bear, watched everything decent on Netflix, and depleted all artistic inspiration. The journal is up to date, and the endless empty days are stretching out ahead for as far as the eye can see. And then further.

7th April 2021

Rummaging around on the net, looking for something to occupy my mind, the Derek Chauvin trial jumped out. It's to be broadcast live on YouTube.

This is it! I thought,

I'm going to follow it and pretend to be a juror!

Problem of lockdown boredom solved, for four weeks anyway!

8th April 2021

Jury duty has begun, and the quality of the bystanders who watched Derek Chauvin squeezing the life out of George Floyd is striking. They were already familiar faces, widely known from the video which had recorded the incident, as they screamed at Chauvin, pleading with him to take his knee off Floyd's neck. But meeting each one of them individually today, their goodness and decency was clear to see.

They all took the stand and were examined and cross-examined as they gave their powerful witness to the murder which they had tried to stop with their voices. It's galling to see Chauvin sitting there watching them, crisp, shaven, suited, and scribbling away in his large notepad, trying to look like a serious pillar of society, as if it were he who was judging them, taking notes on their testimony, in order to later refute it.

He'll be glad of that enormous mask he's wearing.

I'm committed to sticking with this trial, even though restrictions are about to be eased here in the next few days. Greater freedom of movement and meeting is expected, in a limited way, but this job as juror is just too important to ignore. I'm going to sit in on the trial, every day, until it's over.

9th April 2021

As predicted, news on the Covid front is the easing of restrictions. Up to six people from two households can now meet, outside.

It's like being released from prison, solitary confinement actually, and it's hard to handle the excitement!

Meetings galore are crowding my once empty calendar, and first up is Geraldine, now, for coffee at Ollie's. The plan is to discuss our writing work with a reading and feedback session. But let's see what actually happens. Tomorrow it's Rooney, my cold swimming buddy. We'll don our wetsuits, lifejackets and fluorescent tow-floats, and have a swim in the freezing cold water of Loch Lomond, looking up to see the majestic figure of Ben Lomond himself standing over us, sometimes with his head in the clouds. Then we'll wrap up well and cook lunch over the campfire. On Saturday, Don is cooking us one of his fabulous lunches, and on Monday, it's my cousins Lara and Jake, when together we'll eat a plateful of French Fancies and drink Espresso coffee in La Bon Auberge.

A full calendar now!

It's so strange to be making arrangements and meeting up with people again. I haven't seen anyone at all since Christmas day – that's almost four months ago now, four months of solitary confinement, and even then, we had only one very short day off in the long lockdown which had begun in the autumn.

I wonder how people are changing because of these restrictions. The number of people suffering mental health crises is definitely on the rise, especially amongst those who, like me, are prone to depression, and it's almost certain that mental health as a whole is taking a battering. Who knows if life will ever really return to normal?

But more positively, it seems that the vaccine roll-out in Britain has been quite a success so far, and Clare, whose opinion as a Medic is second to none, feels that we'll have a relatively normal summer. I agree. A long summer of sunshine and freedom, but then come autumn, who knows what devastating mutants will have evolved to crush us all yet again.

While the vast majority of people can't wait to get their first and then their second doses of the vaccines, so that we can get back to normal, there's a growing number of people who have begun protesting against them, claiming that Bill Gates and his cohorts are injecting the population with some kind of microchips in order to monitor them.

Rumours of how Gates has already begun experimenting with these microchips, injecting them surreptitiously into the poor in third world countries, are running rampant, as are claims that the virus itself is just a hoax, generated by those faceless, nameless people who already own the planet. It's the ideal way for them to tighten their grip on the world's population and gain for themselves even more power and control, or so the rumours say.

All kinds of extreme conspiracy theories are popping up on social media and gathering strength here in Britain and around the world, and more and more people are taking to the streets to march in protest against the lockdowns and the vaccines.

Groups in the tens of thousands are regularly demonstrating, with their banners and placards reading, ***Freedom of Speech is our Right***, and ***Covid-19 is a HOAX,*** and ***Masks are Muzzles*** and ***Stop G7 and the NEW WORLD ORDER***, and ***Tell the truth – no more fake pandemic*** and ***CONvid Hoax***, and so on.

And as the rumours continue to spread, and the protesters become loud and vociferous, more and more people are refusing to be vaccinated.

18th April 2021

So tired today, and glad not to be on jury duty. It's been a weird week, starting when an artistic competitor back in Spain stomped onto my main sales arena and stole my domain name, slapping his own name over it! Barry Bland. Cheeky wee monkey. Incensed, I sent him a very polite message, concealing my outrage under a blanket of nicety.

My dear Barry, the note said, have only just noticed that you've taken my domain name and put your own name over it. Would you mind changing this please, and maybe coming up with something which is a bit more unique to you?

A long delay before he replied, and then an anodyne excuse, saying that he hadn't intended to use my name, that he was just in the early stages of setting things up, and that he planned to change it.

Hmm.

The images which he had been posting looked very familiar, and I decided to Google them. And there they were. All of them. He had been filching other people's photos, copying them in minute photographic detail, and then posting them, under my domain name, as his own original artworks. Galling! I contacted a photographer friend working in the same area, and asked if she'd heard of him.

Oh yes, she wrote, I blocked him a few years ago - he had been stealing my images. He's a creep.

That was it. Again I wrote to the bold Barry, asking him what he thought he was playing at, stealing my name and other people's photos. No reply, and so I blocked him. But the episode led to a stress reaction, and that horrendous state which hadn't been triggered since Henry of Sterling Renovations was back again.

I took a tranquilliser and waited for Geraldine to appear on the Zoom screen for our weekly writing session. When she appeared, I could see that she too was agitated.

What's wrong? I asked her.

I'm changing my meds she replied, and it's left me on edge.

Geraldine had suffered from bipolar disorder since the age of thirteen, Bipolar One, the worst version of the disorder, and oh my God, how she had suffered for years before diagnosis was made and treatment begun. She still suffered, and though medicines and therapy had helped her to manage the condition, this current lockdown was proving to be a huge challenge to the balance she'd achieved, and she'd recently begun blaming her medication.

She told me that her current meds were leaving her with a foggy mind, an increased appetite, and a weight gain problem, and so she was changing them. Pleading with her not to do anything like that without consulting her psychiatrist was useless. She was adamant that the meds had to be changed.

And then I blurted out my own distress to her.

Because she herself was already on edge, she had a big reaction to what the bold Barry had done, and now we were both in a state, and the idea of writing for twenty minutes in silence was abandoned. Geraldine came round to the house with Pluto. We stood in the living room and just stared at each other, and then began laughing hysterically. Two beautiful women, slightly off balance, and teetering around on the edge of a lockdown meltdown...

It was a glorious, warm, sunny day, and so we went into the garden and lit a fire, not because we needed the warmth of it, but just for the pure magical elemental flying of spark and flame, which seemed to give some expression to the pent-up frustration and manic energy which had been stirred up and was burning in us both. Lockdown. We weren't allowed to sit inside together anyway.

With the warmth of the sun and the fire and each other's slightly unbalanced company, chilled white wine began to seem like a good idea. As we discussed it, and the fact of my tendency to overdo it where fine white wine was concerned, we decided it was better not to. We chatted for a while longer, and then we discussed it again. It began to seem like a good idea to get and drink just the one bottle, a *Sauvignon Blanc*, straight from the fridge of the 10 o'clock Shop. We hopped into the car, got the bottle, and returned to the garden and the still blazing fire.

I had no wine glasses, being by now a strictly one brandy before bed drinker, so Geraldine had her wine from an empty jam jar, and I had mine from a big floral coffee mug. Oh, my goodness, but it was delicious. We sipped and talked and laughed so loudly that the neighbours began peeping out through their curtains to see what the commotion was ... Had a herd of hyenas escaped from the local zoo?

The more they peeped, the more we squealed with laughter. Everything was funny - every word, every gesture, every comment became more hilarious than the last, until eventually we were rolling about on the grass, clutching our bellies, and gasping for breath.

We were quite shocked to notice that the bottle of *Sauvignon Blanc* had become empty. I held it up into the air, squinting at it in the sunshine, just to make sure that there was nothing left in the bottle. Then we looked at each other in horror. How could it be finished? We'd had only a jar or two each, and we were only an hour into conversation. It was just after two o'clock, and the whole beautiful sunny afternoon in the garden stretched out before us.

Maybe we should get another bottle, I said, and Geraldine's eyes lit up.

Well, only one more, she said, emphasising the word *one*.

Oh yes, I replied, definitely only one more, and then that's it.

We donned our masks, mine a pretty floral one with white flowers on a black background which Clare had gotten from Etsy, and Geraldine's, a thick white utilitarian one from the box by the door, abandoned there after all the pretty ones now on the market had become available.

19th April 2021

Today is the final day in the Derek Chauvin trial and I must say, it's a relief that it's coming to a close. It has been quite exhausting, sitting as a juror, albeit a self-appointed one, watching and listening from the living room couch. I have, of course, reached a verdict, and can only hope that my fellow jurors in America will concur.

This final week of the trial saw the Defence bringing some very shady characters to the stand – Barry Brodd, for example, the Use of Force Expert who had earlier testified for the Defence in the trial of the Chicago Policeman, Jason van Dyke, after he had shot sixteen fatal bullets into seventeen year' old Laquan McDonald. He had seen Laquan walking down the street, carrying a knife, and had opened fire on him.

Brodd had testified in that case that those sixteen shots at almost point-blank range constituted a reasonable use of force.

And without flinching, Brodd testified that Chauvin's knee and body weight on George Floyd's neck for nine and half minutes, four of them after Floyd was unconscious and pulseless, was also a reasonable use of force, and completely in line with Police training. This, of course, was in direct contradiction to the testimony given by the Minneapolis Chief of Police and their own Use of Force Trainer, both of whom had testified the previous week.

To the shock of the Prosecution team, Brodd then went on to state that, from what he could see in the video, Floyd had been, and I quote, "resting comfortably in the prone position" under Chauvin's knee, as he lay on the tarmac, pleading for his life, and being slowly asphyxiated.

Then the Defence called a South African pathologist, another mercenary I thought, unkindly, who testified that Floyd had died of exhaust fume inhalation, enlarged heart and Fentanyl ingestion. His testimony seemed so partisan and lacking in any consideration of the circumstances of Floyd's death that Martin Tobin, the world-renowned icon on how we breathe, contacted the Prosecution, and asked to be brought back to refute the pathologist's testimony.

After some debate, and the threat from Eric Nelson to declare a mistrial, Doctor Tobin was allowed back to give some limited testimony, and during his time on the stand he demolished the pathologist's claims.

That man is my hero. A lovely Irishman from a wee village outside Dublin, he had decided early in his medical career to prove that those who said that everything to know about the respiratory system is known, were wrong.

I thought it would be fun, he chuckled from the stand, to find out more 'stuff'.

The result of his endeavours is the fifteen hundred page scientific tome, known throughout the world as *The Bible of Breathing*. Because of Doctor Tobin, we do now live in an age when almost everything about breathing is known.

The Defence also called a retired Emergency Room nurse who had seen Floyd on a previous hospital admission. At that time, he had been arrested and was under the influence of Fentanyl. This nurse appeared to be a bit intoxicated herself on the stand, and she struggled to stick to answering the questions posed. She wanted to discredit Floyd for some reason of her own, but failed to provide anything of any substance to back up her 'feelings'.

But it was clear that she hadn't liked him, and she seemed unable to put her personal feelings aside, and stick to the facts.

As a witness, she seemed to fail the Defence team, providing even more credibility to the Prosecution.

The Defence felt paltry, poor, short lived, and only provided by a few witnesses. Most of them appeared a bit shifty to me, lacking the character and integrity seen in those speaking for the Prosecution.

This afternoon here, this morning in America, both Defence and Prosecution will make their closing statements and the Jury will be sequestered until they reach their verdicts on all three charges – Murder in the Second Degree, Murder in the Third Degree, and Manslaughter.

Quite coincidentally, another incidence of Police brutality towards African-Americans happened on the last day of the trial. Just as the Court was winding up its business, a Policewoman, only miles from the Courtroom, shot dead an eighteen-year-old Afro-American boy during a traffic stop. Apparently, he had hung an air freshener on his rear-view mirror, and the Policewoman felt that this was obstructing his view.

The boy is dead now, killed at point blank range by a single bullet from her Glock. The Policewoman apparently mistook it for her taser.

20th April 2021

All over the news today there are reports coming out of India, telling us that a new mutant of the virus has suddenly appeared there, and that cases are soaring – two hundred thousand new cases, every day, for the past few days. Early suspicions are that this new variant is responsible for the surge in infections.

A lockdown is about to be imposed throughout that huge country, and newsreel footage is showing massive numbers of people descending on the train and bus stations.

These pictures emerging from stations in Delhi and Bombay are astonishing, with the public transport hubs being overwhelmed by the numbers of daily labourers desperate to reach their villages before curfew. Buses can be seen pulling away from the throngs of humanity still trying to board them, despite their being already jam-packed with crowds, all crushed together, inside, on the roof, and hanging from every window and door.

And the trains are the same – there is not one square inch of the departing trains which aren't crammed full of people, with others hanging onto them for dear life, as they pull away from the stations.

But while India's cases are soaring, here the numbers continue to fall, and plans to reopen on the twenty-sixth, six days from now, remain in place. So only one week from today, shops and restaurants will reopen in a limited and cautious way, and Don, Clare, Clare's mum, and I are booked into our favourite Italian restaurant on the South Side for lunch.

We had all been looking forward to this grand

reunion so much for so many weeks, but news of the devastation taking place in India has put something of a damper on my celebrations.

21st April 2021

I watched the summing up arguments in the Derek Chauvin trial yesterday.

Eric Nelson, the annoying Defence attorney, threatened mistrial yet again, but his moan was batted away by Judge Cahill. Nelson spent more than three hours droning on, repeating all his well-worn arguments, stultifying the Jury and the world with his determination to instill the idea of *reasonable doubt* into the weary jurors.

There really should be no debate about it. Chauvin is clearly guilty of Murder in the Second Degree. Anyone who has watched the video knows this.

But Nelson tried to claim that Floyd had died, not because of Chauvin and his offending knee crushing the life breath out of him, but because he had an enlarged heart.

Mr. Blackwell, for the State, concluded his rebuttal with the words, *Mr. Floyd did not die because his heart was too big. He died because Mr. Chauvin's heart was too small.*

I liked that.

Clare told me this morning that despite everything Don, who is very often right about things, still thinks Chauvin will get off because the Americans are mad. Quite mad. Seventy-four million of them, he said, believed, still believe, everything that Donald Trump said, so what hope is there?

I said that if Chauvin gets off, all hell will break loose, not just in Minnesota, but all across the United States of America. And even if he is convicted, that irritating man, Eric Nelson, is sure to shout about a mistrial.

On the Covid front, I've been dying to get the second dose of the vaccine so that I can begin to feel safe again and stop creeping around, avoiding contact with people on my daily walk. So, having concocted a cunning plan yesterday, I went to the greetings card box and fished out the nicest one I could find.

I wrote out a sweet message on the card, bought some chocolates and a nice bunch of Spring flowers, and made my way up to the vaccination centre to hand them into the Vaccination Angels, as I called them on the outside of the envelope.

Inside the card, I expressed my thanks to the vaccination team in glowing terms, and then added a postscript saying that, should they happen to find themselves with a spare vaccine or a cancelled appointment, I could be there in five minutes for my second dose, and this would make sure no dose went to waste.

Most annoyingly, the centre was closed and there was no indication of when it would reopen. Damn it.

22nd April 2021

Yesterday was a strange day for me, being, as it was, the first weekday in a month or so when I was not on jury duty, and I found myself at quite a loss. Painting is my default setting, and so I set about working on the photographs I had taken on Friday, whilst walking with Linda in Bellahouston Park.

This had been our first in-person meeting after months of Zoom chats, and it was such a delight. We walked from her community house, located in a quiet, leafy cul-de-sac on the southside, along a little concealed pathway, and turned right at the end of it – the path to Bellahouston. Had we chosen to turn left, we would have ended up in Pollock, another enormous and stunningly beautiful park, which houses the Burrell Collection as well as the stately Pollock House, which has its own world class collection of Spanish art.

As we walked and chatted, I noticed how joyful the people whom we met seemed to be. The sun was shining, the day was warm, the trees were glorious in their tender April green leaves, and the air was infused with the perfume of new life and happiness. Lockdown was coming to an end, slowly but surely, and everyone was ready to embrace it.

I took many photographs from on top of the high hill looking down into the valley below, where the soldierly lines of uniform trees were casting their long bluish-purple shadows across the pathways, and when we reached the outdoor seating area at the House for an Art Lover, designed by Charles Rennie Mackintosh, I was taken by the liveliness of the people gathered there, standing in small groups drinking coffee and chatting, or sitting at the wooden picnic tables.

One small group seated there seemed to be a particularly colourful *tableaux vivant* of joy, three of them, all snuggling in together, sipping hot drinks from thermos cups, speaking quietly, but with great animation. I asked their permission before clicking, and they were thrilled that their reunion was being captured by a complete stranger.

The photos I got were superb, and one of them in particular has become the inspiration for my latest painting. The gorgeous young Caribbean man with long thick dreadlocks flowing down his back, all the way to his waist, is the star of the piece.

I wish I had taken their details so that I could send them an image of the painting. I think they'd be thrilled that their reunion has been immortalised in vibrant paint and inks.

Later, as I was WhatsApp chatting with Clare to the background sounds of Al Jazeera live, a news flash appeared on the laptop screen,

The verdict in the Derek Chauvin trial is expected in the coming hours.

I leant forward, shocked and excited. Had they really reached a verdict so quickly? What did the speed of this indicate? Good or bad news?

One thing was certain, whatever the verdict was, it was unanimous, otherwise they couldn't be ready to declare. I started to feel quite euphoric – an agreement after only ten hours of deliberation must surely indicate a guilty verdict! But then I remembered the OJ Simpson trial. Four hours it took that Jury, to find that creep innocent. I didn't know what to think. I feverishly messaged Clare. She whooped, declaring it must be guilty if it's so quick! Then I told her about OJ.

Oh God, she wrote, let's hope it's not another OJ situation.

I was becoming over-excited, as is my wont, and had butterflies in my stomach when the next newsflash appeared on the screen,

The Jury has reached and is ready to declare its verdict in the Derek Chauvin murder trial.

Oh God.

I didn't know what to do with myself.

I ran out to the 10 o'clock Shop for a bottle of red wine in order to celebrate what I hoped would be a return of Guilty. I told the shopkeeper and assistants that the Jury had reached a verdict. They just looked at me, blankly.

What? they said.

The Chauvin trial, I replied, they've reached a verdict!

What's the Chauvin trial? they asked.

Oh, never mind, I said, picking up the wine and rushing home in the hope that I hadn't missed the announcement.

I hadn't. The first few sips of the dark red wine warmed my gullet and sent calming waves of intoxication up from the pit of my belly I began to relax, and the madly firing thoughts and feelings abated enough for me to pay attention to the newsreader.

It took several hours before we were allowed back into the Heppin County Courtroom again, where we found the Judge, the invisible Jury, the Prosecution and Defence teams and Derek Chauvin himself, already gathered. The Judge, looking serious behind his Perspex screen, removed his mask and spoke.

Has the Jury reached a verdict? he asked?

We have, said a disembodied voice, and a sealed envelope was handed to Judge Cahill. He opened it quickly, and equally quickly and without drama or fuss, he read aloud the contents.

On the first count, Murder in the Second Degree, we find the defendant guilty; on the second count, Murder in the Third Degree, we find the defendant guilty; on the third count, Manslaughter, we find the defendant guilty.

Oh my God! A hat trick of guilt! A hat trick of justice!

The roar from the crowd outside the Courtroom

almost blew the roof off and the walls down. The camera had remained on the face of Chauvin as the verdicts were read, and above his enormous mask, his eyes darted from side to side as the weight of the words bore down on him, and he struggled to comprehend their meaning.

Guilty.

On all three charges.

He was going away for a long, long time.

The Proecution attorney stood up and spoke, requesting that Chauvin's bail be revoked and that he be immediately imprisoned. The motion was granted, and as the officer behind Chauvin handcuffed him, he turned to Eric Nelson, his attorney, who whispered something to him quickly before he was led away to Oak Park Heights maximum security jail, to await sentencing of up to seventy-five years.

I'll bet Nelson whispered 'mistrial'. He had been setting this up throughout, and I guess it will be his next move.

I felt such relief. It feels like such a landmark verdict, maybe a watershed moment for race relations in America. I felt joy and I felt hope that a better world might be birthing itself, a more just one, a one in which all humanity is honoured and valued and treated with dignity.

From the scenes of jubilation outside the Courtroom, where George Floyd's young daughter was seen rising from her knees and blessing herself before collapsing into the arms of her aunt, the cameras switched to the press conference going on in another part of the city.

Keith Ellison, the Minnesota Attorney General, stood at the microphones, flanked by the Prosecution team. He spoke eloquently, powerfully, praising the courage of the young girl who had pressed record on her mobile phone, capturing the video footage which almost certainly ensured Chauvin's conviction.

He mentioned every single person in what he called *The Bouquet of Humanity* who had stood witness to the crime, and who had cried out, over and over again, trying to stop it, before it was too late.

He spoke well. He gave voice to what many around the world, including myself, were feeling, and there was a great satisfaction in his words. They brought peace and closure.

The News cameras then returned to the studio, where it was announced that just as the verdict was being read, a Police officer in Ohio had shot and killed an Afro-American teenage girl who had appeared to be about to stab another girl.

24th April 2021

Oh my God, India! India, my love! How you are suffering. Fourth day in a row India has experienced record numbers of Covid cases. Three hundred and fifty thousand recorded today, and the peak is not expected for several more weeks.

I watched Alex Crawford's news report on Sky, filmed outside a large hospital in India's capital city, New Delhi. Both inside and outside of the hospital, the scenes were of anguished chaos. Inside the hospital, dead bodies, dead only for the lack of oxygen, were strewn on the floors, and outside, relatives stood in shock with their sick loved ones, watching them gasp helplessly for breath, and then die.

They screamed their rage at the lack of help, their anguish at the loss of their mother, or father, or sister or brother. Just beyond the gates of the hospital, local residents have set up a makeshift crematorium, and as hundreds of funeral pyres are burning and billowing black smoke, every minute another body is brought to the site.

Men with wheelbarrows, scouring the city for wood, are seen weaving in and out of the crematorium like busy worker ants, dumping their fuel for the fires and making their way out again to gather more. This has been going on day and night without cease for days now, and the peak is not expected for another month.

The reasons for this huge and sudden spike are not clear, but the recent *Kumbh Mela* festival in Haridwar, just a few miles down the Ganges from Delhi, had more than ten million devotees in crowded attendance, and, as only a few percent of people are vaccinated so far, it is likely that many super-spreaders were at the festival.

Another reason being suggested and blamed on the Prime Minister, Narendra Modi, is the number of recent political rallies which have been held, a lot of which he himself has headed. In many areas, local elections are taking place, and the politicians in election areas seem to be telling people that there is no Covid19.

Much of the blame is being placed on these political parties for their heedless rallies, and within the political parties themselves, there is squabbling over which of them is to blame for hindering the supply of oxygen to rival states. In a landmark case today, the High Court ruled that if anyone is found to be hindering the supply of oxygen, then they will face the death penalty.

In Delhi itself there are no elections, and so the media is allowed access to show the terrifying spread.

It seems that there are several Covid variants in play, and many are claiming that the British variant has come and mutated in India, causing this dreadful spike.

Many residents of Delhi are lining up outside shops to buy their own oxygen cylinders and treating their relatives at home, being fearful of taking them to a hospital which cannot cope and does not have the oxygen supply needed to keep them alive.

What is being seen in Delhi these last few days is probably only the tip of an enormous iceberg, because there are no statistics, no news coverage, no reporting from India's hundreds of thousands of outlying villages. As Mahatma Gandhi said,

India is not to be found in her few cities, but in her seven hundred thousand villages, and we have hardly ever stopped to enquire as to whether or not they have sufficient to feed and clothe themselves.

And today, so long after the death of Gandhi, no-one is stopping to enquire as to how they are coping with Covid19. Only time will tell.

25th April 2021

The situation unfolding in India is so distressing. Today's reports are saying that things are becoming increasingly dire there, and that over half a million new cases are expected each day. This news coverage is starting to affect me, starting to bring flooding back all the memories of the years I spent there.

My love affair with India began way back in 2006. It was during a deeply troubled time for me, a time when undiagnosed and untreated post-traumatic stress syndrome often left me distressed, anxious and depressed, and it had brought me to the brink of suicide. During those times, I had been able to find some comfort in prayer and spiritual reading, and it was through this reading that I came to know the writings of a man known as Brother Magnus, who had been the spiritual teacher in Shanthi Ashram in the south of India.

In the deepest darkest hour, when the will to live had left me and the desire to die had grown so strong that I was ready to leave this world, it was the image of Brother Magnus, his hands reaching down to me through thick black billowing clouds of suffocating despair, beckoning me, inviting me into his home in Shanthi Ashram, which brought me back from the dead, so to speak. This ashram was the place where he had taught and guided others through their pain and confusion and desperation, and it was the place in which the alchemical magic in his own soul was to blossom into the thousand-petalled lotus.

It was through his strength and the light which he sent me that I was eventually able to surrender my despair to God, and get up from the bed, and chose. And I chose life. I chose life over death; I chose hope over fear; I chose love over despair. I chose, and in choosing, my love for his soul ever rises upwards in grateful thanks.

In the days and weeks which followed on from this brush with death, I focussed my mind solely on getting to Shanthi. I searched the internet for websites which might give me information on where exactly it was, and how I could get there.

Eventually I found the website, and wrote to Brother Joseph, the spiritual teacher who had followed on after Magnus's death, some ten years previously.

After an email exchange back and forth between us, I was eventually given permission to come to the ashram for a long stay, to paint and write and participate in the community's diet of prayer. I could stay for six months, I was told, and the ashram would send a car to the airport to collect me.

It is hard now, so many years later, to recall the joy which this message from Brother Joseph brought me. My soul somehow knew that this visit would lead me into a new stage of life, and a renewal of hope.

Shortly after I received his correspondence, I began a period of intense activity. Firstly, I handed in my notice at my teaching job, and began working furiously to make sure that all the students were up to date and up to the mark for their exams. Satisfied that everything was in order for them, I then contacted some letting agencies, chose one of them, and arranged to rent out my apartment.

Eventually the day of my departure arrived, a bitter cold January morning, and, laden with luggage and an enormous suitcase filled with art materials, my sister Beth dropped me at Glasgow Airport, and we waved each other a tearful goodbye.

I flew first to Colombo in Sri Lanka, where the airline had arranged a beach resort stopover for three days. I was truly grateful for this unexpected holiday, for it allowed time and space to reflect on all that I had just left behind, and the chance to prepare for this new stage of life. When the three days were over, we were taken back to the airport to board the next flight for Madurai, the airport closest to the ashram.

True to his word, Brother Joseph had sent two young Indian men, boys really, to meet me, and I was so relieved to see them standing just outside the terminal building, smiling broadly, and holding a large white card with my name clumsily scrawled on it. They took my luggage, and we all clambered into an ancient rickety Ambassador car to begin the hour-long drive to the ashram.

I died a thousand deaths on that journey. The traffic chaos was beyond description, and time after time as we pelted along, the Ambassador charging headlong towards truck and car and rickshaw, only to veer off to safety at the last minute, I screamed and tried to speak to the driver, to beg him to slow down, to stay on his own side of the road. But he spoke no English. He just turned and flashed his huge bright white teeth and smiled at me, and kept his foot down on the pedal.

Shaken and drenched in sweat, I finally arrived at Shanthi Ashram. I had been longing for the peace and tranquillity and silence of this retreat for many months, and the sight of the sign on the main road leading to its entrance was the answer to a long-held prayer. We turned from the asphalt road, onto a bumpy dirt track, and shuddered along for a few minutes before turning left into the ashram proper.

I was shocked at the sight. Rather than an oasis of peace and tranquillity, what awaited me was a full-blown jamboree of festival music, dancing women in exotic saris, men clapping and chanting, long-suffering cows and bulls and oxen, garlanded and daubed with bright red bhindis in the middle of their foreheads, fires lit and burning, on top of them cauldrons of food bubbling in the midday heat. Brother Joseph was there to greet me, along with Brother Yesudas, whom I was later to discover was something of a sparkling diamond of a man, but with some rough, as yet unpolished, edges.

And that was how my long sojourn in India began, with my arrival at the ashram, slap bang in the middle of the *Pongal* Festival celebrations.

26th April 2021

Just back from our first post lockdown lunch, in a restaurant, with people! Jerry took Don, Clare, and I out for a fabulous meal at our favourite restaurant, Oro, on the south side of the city, where we revelled in each other's company, conversation and the fine Italian food which is always served there.

We had our usual seasoned focaccia topped with succulent chopped tomatoes, covered in oregano and mixed herbs, as a shared starter, Don and I dipping ours into lashings of thick inky-black balsamic vinegar and virgin olive oil. I followed this with meatballs in a spicy tomato sauce on long spaghetti, smothered in fresh parmesan and black pepper, and ended it all with a hot chocolate brownie topped with boozy purple red cherries and vanilla ice-cream. Delish!

I made the most of the occasion, dressing up in a floor length summer dress from John Lewis –a floaty chiffon number –white fabric decorated in red roses, with a daring slash down the back, and a set of Keshi pearls and earrings. To complete the outfit, I had draped a pink velveteen cape over my shoulders, and, with matching pink elbow length gloves, which Jerry gave me for Christmas some years ago, my over-the-top post-lockdown outfit was complete.

I knew it was over the top, but I didn't care! Lockdown was over, and I was going to make the most of it. At least no-one asked if I was out for Hallowe'en.

When I got home, I heard from Annika. She says that the whole of India is in Covid-chaos – what we're seeing on the news here from Delhi does not begin to describe what is happening all over the country as a whole.

Oh God.

27th April 2021

Airship loads of medical equipment from Britain have arrived in India and are being dispersed by long trains which are snaking the length and breadth of the country, dropping off supplies. More equipment is en-route from America.

The situation is absolutely dire. Mr. Tedros Adhanom, Head of the World Health Organisation, has described it as 'beyond heart-breaking', and alarm is just growing and growing as it becomes clear that the problem is a doubly mutated strain of the virus. So far, it has proven impervious to medicines and, worst of all, no vaccine can prevent infection, or curtail its spread.

Desperate.

We can be sure that this ultra-strong, doubly mutated strain won't confine itself to the subcontinent. I wonder how long we have before it arrives here, before we're back in a full lockdown.

Unsurprisingly, the Government in Britain is in disarray again, fighting off claims that our Prime Minister has said in private that he will see bodies piled high in the streets rather than impose another lockdown, a claim which he has, of course, denied, making me feel all the more certain that he did in fact say it.

More sleaze allegations are on the go at the moment too, and include the accusation that he sought and gained funds from party cronies to pay the sixty thousand pound refurbishment costs for his flat at Downing Street, because his fiancée couldn't bear "the John Lewis nightmare" installed by Teresa May.

What the hell's wrong with John Lewis? I thought, as I sat in my John Lewis nightie and dressing gown on my John Lewis sofa.

What the hell is wrong with John Lewis?

28th April 2021

Twenty-five more makeshift crematoria have sprung up in vacant lots around Delhi, and even still, they cannot cope with the mounting numbers of dead. Bodies are being burned in gardens and on the streets and sidewalks, and outside hospitals. In other places, bodies which cannot be burned are being piled high outside the new crematoria.

The darkest chapter in Covid19s short history is unfolding in Delhi, and it is feared that the situation in the outlying villages is even worse. It is estimated that only one tenth of cases and deaths are contained in the official statistics.

The scenes of burning bodies and piles of dead are truly appalling, apocalyptic, and the worst is still weeks away.

29th April 2021

These scenes of horror coming out of India keep bringing the memories back, the memories of all the wonder-filled years I spent in that most incredible of countries.

I remember the shock of arriving at Shanthi, in the midst of the exuberant Pongal celebrations, and being led to a tiny hut by Chitty Babu, Brother Joseph's right-hand man – a very bright, cheerful young man, built like a boxer and very strong. He carried my heavy suitcases with ease as he led the way, turning round every so often to flash me a big smile and a chuckle and to mutter something completely unintelligible but very endearing.

We walked past the cowsheds where lean, almost naked young men were carrying and dumping large bales of hay, while others swept and washed the big shed and hosed down the cows. We walked past the banana grove and papaya trees, groaning under the weight of their huge plump fruits, past coconut trees and vibrant flowering shrubs, and eventually we came to the hut. Chitty Babu produced a key from the breast pocket of his chequered cotton shirt and swiftly unlocked the padlock, opening the door to what was to be my home for the next six months.

It was tiny, and furnished with a hard wooden cot which was to torture my body in the days ahead, a small sky-blue wooden table, and a rickety wooden chair. There was an ancient ramshackle cupboard for storage, an inset bookshelf and, through a small doorless doorway, lay the toilet. Chitty Babu placed my suitcases, which virtually filled the space, inside, laughing loudly at some unseen joke, and, wobbling his head vigorously, he backed out of the space, leaving me alone in the hut.

I just stood there on the bare concrete floor and stared.

After some time had passed, I ventured through the opening and into the bathroom. Everything was done in concrete, seemed to have been moulded in concrete, and rising up out of the concrete floor was a kind of a wall-length concrete banquette, halfway along which was a cracked, coverless plastic toilet seat, set askew over a big black hole. I peered down into the hole. There was water in it, far down, and a strange smell, like mothballs.

Beside the hole lay a metal bucket with a handle, and off to one side was a tiny, cracked washbasin and tap, and next to this, sticking out of the wall, was another tap. Below this second tap there was a huge psychedelic plastic bucket, inside which was a small multi-coloured plastic jug, and just off in the corner and on the floor, there was one big heavy stone.

I picked up the stone to have a look, and then ran screaming in horror out of the bathroom, out of the hut and onto the veranda. Brother Joseph was just then passing by, and he saw me.

Manee, Manee, he said, what is wrong with you?

Inside, I gasped. Creatures. Hundred of
creatures. Crawling all over the bathroom.

Brother Joseph lifted his long white cotton dhoti

above his ankles, shuffled off his sandals, and made his way through the hut and into the bathroom.

What is wrong? he asked.

Underneath that stone, I replied. Creatures.

He moved the stone with his bare foot, and we both watched as a hundred black squirming things of all different shapes and sizes wriggled and swarmed, running for cover.

Brother Joseph looked at me, and said,

Manee, Manee! These are all God's creatures, all of them, and you must love them.

With that, he lifted the hems of his dhoti, put his sandals back on, and floated off down the ashram paths.

30th April 2021

For my first six weeks or so at Shanthi, I wandered around like Alice in Wonderland. Everything was so bright, colourful, so vibrant and bursting with life, not only the trees, heavily laden with all kinds of exotic fruits, not only the flowers, bursting with life, and the exotic birds and peacocks and butterflies, but the people themselves, with their brightly flashing smiles and perfect pearly white teeth, were also bursting with life, despite the poverty, despite the relentless grind to earn enough as a daily labourer to buy the rice and daal and vegetables which was their staple, to find enough firewood to cook their meal.

It was such a change from Drumnock, where grey-faced people moved around slowly in a greyscale landscape, eating too much and not enjoying it, drinking too much, and becoming bloated as they huddled against the wind, the rain, the cold. This was a whole new world, and I was drinking it all in, in wonderment.

And it was loud. Very loud. My senses were daily assailed by new sounds – the song of a beautiful long-tailed bird which I loved, and which wakened me each morning, the labourers shouting instructions to one another in Tamil, the music from the village, and new sights, and new smells from flowers and from the cooking with herbs and spices I did not know, the heady incense, the strange aroma of the beedis, which some of the workers smoked.

The ashram had a daily routine around prayer times, beginning at five in the morning with *Nama Japa* in the temple, and ending with *Nama Japa* again at nine in the evening. This evening *Nama Japa* was my favourite time.

The temple, a Hindu design, was open to the elements from waist height and covered with a brush roof. You could sit there, cross-legged in the evening, chanting the praise of the name of the Lord, rocking back and forth gently, and gazing at the moon and stars, hypnotised, pacified, transported magically into another world, and a new dimension.

We lived the life of the very poor – rudimentary accommodation, cheap simple food, no luxuries, and I loved it. The food may have been cheap and simple, but the skill of the cooks from the village, two beautiful sari-clad women, Julie and Papita, made the humble ingredients into the most delicious of meals. I ate well and was satisfied.

After midday prayer and lunch, we were free until three thirty in the afternoon, when all the ashram guests would gather in the tea circle for tea and chat, before Brother Joseph's daily talk began at four o'clock.

I got to know people from all over the world at that tea circle, people who had loved Brother Magnus's teaching and had travelled as a kind of pilgrimage, and for spiritual retreat and nourishment. Some stayed only a few days, some for a few weeks, and then me, who was staying for six months.

I hadn't realised it at the time, but my arrival there in mid-January was the peak time for foreign visitors, and so the ashram was very full and very busy. By the time I left, I was the only guest. I was also twenty pounds lighter.

1st May 2021

May has arrived in Drumnock. The days are longer and brighter and often filled from start to end with warmth in the sunshine but a cold nip in the shadows; the trees are fattening up with their cloaks of leaves as the ever-busy birds flit in and out of their shelter, adding the final touches to their nests as they await the arrival of their young. Flowers are blossoming and opening, and my wee postage stamp of a garden is filled with bluebells.

Nature is trumpeting her happiness here, and our grey world of lockdown is beginning to warm and brighten again.

Jenny, an ArtClub buddy, captured a shot of a coots' nest, erected on a tree stump in the middle of the Bingham Hotel's pond. Sitting atop the splendid structure in the water and in her nest, Mrs. Coot is carefully arranging the yellow and orange daffodils her mate brought home to decorate their abode.

On the Covid front, the vaccine programme here is on target, and the number of cases continues to fall. Yesterday, there were only twenty-two deaths in the whole of Britain.

But India is in an extreme state of prolonged

suffering and distress. More than five hundred thousand new cases today, and it's reckoned that the true number could be as many as ten times this. Volunteer drivers have begun circulating the streets, collecting dead bodies from houses and apartments, and piling them up outside the many makeshift crematoria which continue to spring up in vacant lots. In these places, where the temperature is in the forties, the blistering hot air is putrid with the smell of burning flesh.

2nd May 2021

Back in Shanthi ashram, as my senses were being startled by all the newness of India, my reasons for being there, for having come to Shanthi Ashram, having fled to Shanthi Ashram to be precise, were not far from the surface of my mind. Life in Drumnock had come to an end. The torture of it was no longer a viable option – it had brought me to such a state of exhaustion and distress and hopelessness that I could not carry on. And I wondered if Shanthi was my future.

At that time, almost fifteen years ago now, I was always seeking signs from God, signs that he was there, that he was active in my life, signs that he was guiding me. One of the signs, a symbol really, which often appeared to me, either through a trick of the light or on a bookshelf, or embedded within a pattern, was the mandorla.

I loved this symbol. It had begun appearing to me long before I knew what it was and what it meant, and before I discovered that it is perhaps the most ancient sacred symbol known to mankind. It is said to have been inscribed on the Ark of the Covenant by the ancient Hebrews as they wandered in the desert, and it is known as the *vesica pisces*, which symbolises the sacred geometrical patterning of all life on Earth.

The symbol itself is one of two intersecting circles in which the intersection forms an almond shape, from which the word 'mandorla' is derived. The symbol has been interpreted in many ways throughout the centuries, and it always describes the interactions and interdependence of opposing dimensions and forces.

But the interpretation which has most meaning for me is the mandorla as the symbol of the intersection of two worlds, the visible and the invisible, the form and the formless, the spiritual and the material, the divine and the human. The early Christians are said to have used the intersected almond shape as their secret sign, because Christ, as both human and divine, fitted perfectly into it.

It also happens to look like a fish.

This was the meaning which, when I discovered it, comforted me most, and assured me that I was not alone.

A more recent symbol, one which had come to me after I had begun planning the flight to India, was concentric circles. It happened one bright afternoon as I sat on the sofa in my apartment, facing the big bay window, and writing in my journal. I was writing with a silver topped pen, and as I wrote I noticed something from the corner of my eye which seemed to be dancing on the back of the sofa where I sat. I turned my head to look, and saw that the sunlight, hitting the top of the silver pen, was casting light onto the fabric.

This light was continuously forming itself into a pulsating pattern of three concentric circles. It seemed to be a living breathing thing, filled with life and vigour. The deep stillness and silence which often descended at moments of communion with the invisible world came over me, and I knew that this was a sign, a message from another dimension, and I took note of it, knowing that its significance would unfold over time. I wasn't to see that symbol again until I sat down on the hard wooden cot in Shanthi Ashram, confused, distressed and utterly lost, and cried.

This symbol, for me, seemed to have something to do with writing, partly because it came through the top of a pen, and partly because writing had already proven to be good medicine. Back in 2003, three years before I left for India, Clare had suggested that I start writing down all that I was feeling, as a kind of release or therapy to help me cope with the anxiety and depression which had become constant companions.

And so I embarked on a journey through writing to explore my past experiences, memories, people, and situations, in an attempt to uncover the roots of whatever it was that ailed me, that had dogged me throughout life, and had prevented me from forming any kind of stable relationship with a potential husband, for I had once wanted to marry and to have children.

This writing exercise quickly took on a life of its own with its own dynamic, and I would often find that, having sat down with a hot drink at eight in the evening to write for half an hour, time had flown by until it was suddenly two in the morning, and fifty more pages had appeared. The exercise never did uncover what ailed me, that wasn't to emerge until I had done several years in India, but it was of enormous benefit, and it helped me hold things together in a way that had eluded me before.

When I arrived in India, what ailed me continued to ail me, and was as much of a mystery as it had ever been. 'It', this mysterious unconscious 'thing', still drove my subconscious mind and governed my feelings and emotions as it had done throughout life, but at least now I found myself in a situation where I could relax and forget about working for a while, forget about the need to earn a living, and give my mind the space and quiet it so desperately needed.

The apartment was in the hands of an agency in the West End – they would rent it out to suitable tenants and send me the monthly rent, minus their commission. With the differing economies of Britain and India, this money represented a handsome income and would more than cover all expenses. And that was a great relief. My mind could relax for a while, and let go of all the usual worries.

I was able to spend my time in the ashram doing more or less as I pleased, and so I spent hours each day painting and writing, a continuation of the journaling exercise, and painting from the unconscious. I would stretch the watercolour paper by soaking a large sheet of it in the huge psychedelic bucket, lifting it out, and then pulling it over a wooden board which Chitty Babu had found for me in the village, taping it with masking tape around the edges. Once dry, I would sit with this canvas in the hut, my eyes closed, and hands spread flat over the paper, and pray.

I wanted the painting to be a healing process, for it to be a conduit for the mystery in my soul to express itself, and this was my prayer. Then I would choose three colours from the box of tubes at random, often through closed eyes, and begin painting. I used sponges at first to make big marks and then, when these marks were pleasing to the eye, I moved into them with brushes, first big ones, and then smaller ones for detail.

At some point during this process, something would begin to emerge on the canvas – the suggestion of a tree, or a flower, a bird, or a fish. When this happened, I would begin to clarify the image until the painting was of a definite tree, or a flower, or a singing bird, or a swimming fish. And then the painting would be complete.

I never called a painting finished until I found it beautiful, and I never gave up on a painting before it reached this stage. As I worked, a mantra formed in my mind and repeated itself continuously during the process,

Every stroke is a stroke of love.

I never knew before beginning a painting what the end result would be, and so each painting was something of a mysterious adventure into the unknown, in order to make it known.

3rd May 2021

This is week four of the Writing Group meet-ups on Zoom, and I'm waiting for the others to arrive. We are now four in number – Jenna is our new member, and today is her first session. I met her only on Friday, when she came to collect a painting, one which I had donated to that wonderful Scottish Charity, *Giveadogabone*, and which Jenna had bought. Months ago. Due to lockdown, she hadn't been able to collect it before now, and I was very relieved that she loved her painting, *A Sunday Afternoon in the Botanicals,* even more in the flesh than she had done online.

We sat out in the garden, me in a John Lewis nightie, dressing gown and socks, hair an unbrushed mop of wave and curl, and Jenna, fresh from her appointment with the beautician. An unlikely pair we were, but we hit it off immediately and could have talked all day. She confessed that she was addicted to beautiful journaling notebooks and had, throughout her life, bought, and kept a number of these. But she had never started writing.

Now is the time, she said, to bite the bullet!

...

Just heard that Geraldine won't make the meeting. She is in hospital. When I woke this morning and checked the mobile, I found that she had been phoning me at all hours through the night. And now her husband, Kevin, has just telephoned to say that she's been admitted to Stobhill Hospital, because of an acute manic episode.

She's been fiddling around with her meds, Kevin said, desperate to stop the brain fog and weight gain. But now she's gone into a full-blown manic episode.

He sounded exasperated on the phone, and I could tell that he was at the end of his tether. He had no idea of how long she would be in hospital, but he did say that she couldn't have contact with the outside world, not until this manic episode had passed.

...

Julie has failed to turn up. Again. She's chasing her tail setting up a new Health Service practice, trying to get the place in order so that she can begin her project of establishing a clinic, one which combines allopathic medicine with holistic therapies.

And now I've just had a WhatsApp message from Jenna. She's with her mother, who is about to be admitted to the Queen Elizabeth Hospital, with Covid. They're waiting on the ambulance. This means that the online Writing Group is now reduced to only one member. Me.

5th May 2021

The early days at Shanthi Ashram were very exciting and I was all agog most of the time, meeting new people, hearing their stories, making new friends. I had learned *Champissage*, a style of Indian head massage, at a course in London shortly before arriving in India, and so I offered this service to all who needed it. I enjoyed having a guest on the veranda, in the shade of the huge banyan tree just beside my hut, stripped to the waist, seated, and drifting off into bliss as I massaged their head, neck, face, shoulders and back.

I offered to massage some of the ashram workers, the women who toiled daily carrying heavy loads on their heads, and often complained of headaches as they sought Paracetamol from the foreign guests, all of whom seemed to have brought an entire medicine cabinet in their luggage. But they were terrified at the thought. And so I just gave them the Paracetamol.

I took to walking into the local town, Kalitooly, each day after lunch. The path led from the back of the ashram, into the eucalyptus forest, along the banks of the now dried Kaveri River, the second most sacred river in India, along past the outdoor crematorium, across a little bridge, and into the bustling town.

Just across the bridge lay the bus station, always

mobbed with people and buses arriving and departing, surrounded by stalls displaying their fresh fruits and vegetables in bright colourful mountains, with bright colourful vendors shouting out to passers-by, their prices, their wares. Cows and goats wandered freely, chomping at garbage from the street, sniffing at the fruits and vegetables on the stalls.

My routine was always the same – a walk through the forest, past the bus station and stalls, and on to a little chai stand, where I would buy a two Rupee metal tumbler of coffee, *sakare vendam*, without sugar, and sit sipping it on the step of the tobacco shop next to the stall.

Then I would return to the ashram along the main road, keeping to the dusty roadside track to avoid being hit by the fast-moving crazy cars, trucks, bullock carts, motorbikes, rickshaws. It wasn't unusual to see a family of six bundled on top of a small motorbike and careening along the road, or to see a motorbike with a cow or a goat tethered to the back seat as a pillion passenger. In time, I became used to all these things and saw nothing odd in them.

I learned a lot about Hinduism, and especially about *Advaita Vedanta*, or non-duality, the highpoint of Hindu philosophy, from Brother Joseph's daily talks in the meditation hall. All the foreign guests would gather there each day after tea circle, and sit cross-legged on a cushion on the floor, or on one of the low hard wooden benches, listening to Brother Joseph describing the development of Hinduism throughout the millennia.

He spoke of it in very human terms, going back to our earliest ancestors, who had once stood in awestruck wonder at the fullness of the world and all it holds – the sun, the moon, the stars, the oceans and seas, and nature, and all of life ...

He described their movement from innocence and wonder at the natural world and all its forms, through their deepening awareness and understanding that there is also a formless, invisible realm. They came to see that it is within this invisible realm that all forms, all *things,* arise. They also saw that the forms which arise only linger for a time, and then they dissolve again, back into the formless, invisible realm from which they arose.

They came to understand this formless realm as Brahman, an aspect of God, and saw it as eternal, unchanging, conscious, infinite, omnipresent, and it became for them the spiritual foundation of the world of form and change. They also saw the world as being shot through with Brahman, and saw Brahman as the core of everything. They realised that we humans, with our unique form of consciousness, had within us an immediate access point to this potent, invisible realm and could directly experience our oneness with it.

It was a philosophy which chimed with the experience of the Christian mystics, with their *unus mundus*, or "one world", in which they live and move and have their being. They directly experience their communion with the underlying reality from which everything comes, and to which it returns, and they call this reality God. But within Hinduism this very same concept is described so fully and in such detail that its meaning becomes crystal clear.

I learned to disentangle this philosophy from its history and development, seeing only the pure truth of it as a description of all life and all human experience.

I had studied Philosophy at University, Moral Philosophy from Plato and Aristotle onwards, and had studied modern Western philosophy, but I had never come across anything so full and so satisfying to the mind and soul as this Indian Philosophy of pure Consciousness, which is what it really is.

Years later, at the Hay Book Festival, I listened to the renowned English Philosopher, A.C. Grayling, giving a talk on his then recently published book, *The History of Western Philosophy*. Grayling recounted the development of philosophy from the ancients, Plato and Aristotle, all the way through to the present-day atheist thinkers like Richard Dawkins, who had recently published, to much critical acclaim, *The God Delusion*.

I was amazed at how shallow and unsatisfying they all were, when compared to Indian philosophy, and so I was pleasantly surprised when Grayling finished his talk by referring to it. He told us that he had just recently heard of *Advaita Vedanta,* or non-duality, done some reading on it, and realised that he must now, at his grand old age of seventy-two, return to the drawing board. That left me feeling hopeful for the future of philosophy in the Western world.

6th May 2021

Just back from voting. Cast both ballots, regional and national, for the Labour Party. Some witty soul posted a sign, a mock-up of the Tory Government's own Covid catchphrase, on Facebook yesterday,

A message for all Tory voters this Thursday: Stay home, save lives, protect the NHS.

I thought that was funny. And true. If the National Health Service ever does die, it will be at the hands of the Tories.

No abating of the horrors in India so far, and now the experts are warning that there will almost certainly be a third wave there, hard on the heels of the current one. This doubly mutated strain, which is causing such havoc in India, has now arrived in Britain. But the numbers of cases and deaths here continue to fall. Only four deaths yesterday.

My friend Annika in India is annoyed at the reportage.

Italy, she said, has a population of sixty million, and one hundred and twenty thousand deaths so far; here in India, with a population of almost one and half billion, we have had two hundred and twenty thousand deaths. But graves, she said, are not as attention grabbing as bodies burning in the streets.

These figures, though, don't seem accurate to me. But she is right – the figures are meaningless, unless they're given as per capita numbers.

7th May 2021

Back in Shanthi Ashram, the days were unfolding into weeks, and as guests came, became brief friends, and then sadly left again, I began to feel like an old hand at ashram life.

I had learned all the Sanskrit chants and the Tamil bhajans and prayers by heart and with perfect pronunciation, and was so proud of this that I would, at prayer times and in the dining hall before and after meals, chant and sing just a bit more loudly than I needed to, so that all the new foreign guests could hear, and be amazed.

Some guests, though, were people who had been returning to Shanthi year after year for up to thirty years. I sought out their company, to listen and learn.

I became friendly with a rather posh English gentleman in his sixties, Alan Harkins. He was tall and lean with snowy white hair, a little white beard, and a moustache. He wore the Kavi coloured robes of the Sanyasi, and he liked to take charge of things whenever he could – overseeing the vegetable washing and chopping after breakfast, and making sure that the big wood fire in the outhouse, which heated the water for our daily bucket bath, was kept lit and burning.

He had been visiting the ashram for more than thirty years, and had known Brother Magnus personally.

Magnus changed his life, he said. You could tell that Alan relished playing the role of the Indian Sanyasi for three months each winter, before returning to his tweeds and his hunting lodge in the Cotswolds come Springtime. I enjoyed his company, and his eccentricity.

One afternoon at tea circle, Alan and I had been chatting about enlightenment, that thing so sought after by Western tourists in Indian ashrams, and the various means of achieving it - the age-old practices of meditation, chanting, silence, fasting, prayer. Alan told me that there was a very interesting and powerful Sadhu living in a small hut just outside the ashram fence, in the eucalyptus forest.

You should speak with him, he said.

Amazed at this startling fact, I made a mental note to visit him as soon as possible.

Don't let the Brothers know that you're going Marney, Alan shouted after me as I left the circle.

I turned round and saw Alan nodding at me meaningfully, in a conspiratorial manner. This sniff of controversy and secrets piqued my interest even more, and I resolved to visit the Sadhu the very next day.

8th May 2021

Something has happened across the road. I can see it from the living room window. There's a big open field there, where boys play football, people walk their dogs, and children enjoy the play park. Since this morning, two Policeman have been there, patrolling a large area which has been cordoned off with Police tape. There's a Police car and van there too. No-one has been allowed to enter the area.

9th May 2021

It was after the first visit to the Sadhu's hut that I fell in love with him. I had never seen such a beautiful creature in my entire life. His glowing presence seemed to extend for yards beyond his physical form, and his physical form itself really was something to behold. He was around six feet tall with a perfectly formed body, visible for all to see, as he dressed only in a Kavi coloured dhoti covering his lower half, and his brownish hair, made golden by the sun, fell around his face and shoulders in bouncing, glimmering curls and ringlets.

His skin was golden brown, supple, and glowing, and his eyes were a deep hazel twinkle in his handsome face. He smiled all the time and laughed at the slightest provocation – a loud, deep, infectious laugh, which was to have me dissolved in uncontrollable laughter myself during our many afternoons together.

When I was leaving after my first visit, he took my face in both his hands and, looking deeply into my soul, he whispered,

I luff you, I luff you.

Oh my God!

My heart was racing, defenses melting away, knees like

putty ...

"I'll bet you say that to all the girls!", I laughed, and ran off through the forest and back to my hut, where I sat on the cot for a long time, in a kind of stupefied daze.

10th May 2021

On some days a tailor would come to the tea circle in the morning, showing swatches of cotton, in various colours and qualities and thread counts, to the guests, along with suggested styles of kurtas, pants, *salwar kameez*. His name was James, and he had been associated with the ashram for decades, and his father before him. I noticed that if any of the Brothers were in the circle when James arrived, they would always make some excuse to leave, so that they never spoke to him.

It seemed strange to me, and so I asked Alan about it.

The story was vague and went back many years, to the days of James's father, when there had been some falling out over money and access to guests, and a feud between the tailor, his family, and the ashram was born. I never did get the full story, but there was a definite air of animosity between the tailor and the Brothers at the ashram.

One day James's son, a strong good looking young man named Kumar, came with his father to the tea circle and began chatting. He was bright and charming, and when he invited me across the road to his charitable foundation offices, I gladly accepted. There was a fellow Irishman visiting, he said, and he wanted me to meet him.

The following morning at ten, Kumar arrived on his motorbike to take me to the village. I hated being a pillion passenger, and as we bounced along over the dirt track, weaving in and out to avoid the biggest bumps, I was certain that I was going to fall off. When we arrived at the offices, constructed from walls of woven palm fronds and covered with a brush roof, I was shown into a little central office, where the Irishman sat, typing at a computer.

Despite the flimsiness of the structures, they had electricity and if not running water, there was an outdoor hand pump which provided plenty of clean, fresh water for chai and cooking, flushing the toilet and washing.

I shook hands with the slender elegant Irishman, who introduced himself, with a wry smile, as Neil Kavanagh, no relation to the famous poet.

12th May 2021

Two men have been arrested for attempting to murder two other men in the field across the road. Both were stabbed and are now fighting for life in the Queen Elizabeth Hospital. The whole incident was caught on CCTV, but footage is not being released as it is said to be 'too gruesome'. The motivation is not known, but the attackers are now in Police custody.

Across the road.

Oh God.

On the Covid front, India's cases dipped briefly for two days, but are now soaring again, with yesterday's totals being the highest so far. The World Health Organisation spokesman has warned that this variant in India is now of global concern, and cases of it are popping up everywhere.

In other news coming out of the Middle East, we hear that in Israel, a massively imbalanced war is taking place. Hamas is responding with rockets to the outrage of Israeli soldiers entering and assaulting worshippers at Friday prayer in the Al Aqsa Mosque in Jerusalem, as well as to Israeli settlers ousting Palestinians from their homes and stealing their houses. Israel, in retaliation, is clobbering Gaza with airstrikes, demolishing large apartment blocks where families live, and justifying their actions with the claim that Hamas has offices there.

It's unbearable.

A Jewish acquaintance of mine, Paul Levy, wrote a very insightful article on the psychology of Israel's behaviour towards its neighbour. In this article, entitled, *Israel Outgassing its Trauma,* Paul goes deep into the history of the Holocaust, the psychology of trauma, and how it plays itself out in the lifetime of the traumatised victim. He then extrapolates from the traumatised individual to the traumatised nation, and the nation of Israel fits the template perfectly. Turning the Gospel's moral guidance on its head, they seem to be doing unto others what has been done unto them.

13th May 2021

Neil Kavanagh, the elegant Irishman, had joined what was, because of his money, a very big charitable foundation in and around the area of Shanthi, and he wanted me to join it. He didn't make that clear, however, until after he had shown me around all the areas in which he was working, and all that he had and was continuing to achieve for some of the poorest people on the planet.

Over many metal tumblers of chai in his tiny office, interspersed with metal platters of cookies, then lunch, then dinner, all served by sari-clad women from the village, he told me his story.

Neil was born in Ireland, just outside Dublin, into a family of potato farmers. The family business did well, producing huge crops of round white tatters which were popular throughout the country. But when Neil's father died, leaving the farm to him, he decided to take a change of direction, and with the help of a chemist friend, he invented what was to become Ireland's favourite potato treat – *Kavanagh's Crunchy Crisps.*

His friend, George Kennedy, who had studied Chemistry at Trinity College Dublin, came up with a recipe and method which made Kavanagh's crisps into the most crunchy on the market. He also added a new flavour, Balsamic Vinegar, which was created by mixing fine grade balsamic vinegar, sourced from Italy and barrel-aged for over twenty-five years, with corn starch, and then power-spraying a fine mist of the mixture onto the cooked crisps.

They were a huge hit, so much so that it became difficult to keep up with demand, and with some investment from the Bank of Ireland, Neil built a huge factory in Dublin, and production of the new potato snacks began on an industrial scale. Within two years, Neil was a millionaire many times over, and his crisps were everywhere to be seen as the Irish munched their way through mountains of *Kavanagh's Crunchy Crisps*.

I was fascinated by Neil's story, and encouraged him to keep talking.

Why India, I asked, why here? Why all this work to help women and girls? Why not men?

Well now, he said, in his delicious Irish brogue, that's another story altogether.

He thought for a while, as his elegant fingers stroked his greying goatee, and then he suggested that I return the following day to pick up the story. He had a meeting now with the village elders, and he didn't want to be late. Kumar, who had been sitting quietly in the background the whole time, stood up to take me to his motorbike for the short ride back to Shanthi.

Thanks Kumar, I said, but I'm okay to walk. Oh, and there's no need to collect me tomorrow – now I know where you are, I'll find you again.

Not going on that bike again, I thought, as I trailed the dusty paths which led to home, reaching there in time for evening prayer.

14th May 2021

The Indian variant has arrived in Britain, and is spreading in London, Bolton, and Glasgow. Just as this announcement was being made, the UK Immigration Office sent Police cars and vans into the Glasgow Covid hotspot to remove two illegal immigrants who have been living there for more than ten years.

They caused uproar as the neighbours, numbering around one thousand, came out onto the street, surrounded the Immigration Control van which held their two Punjabi neighbours, and chanted,

Leave our neighbours alone!

One man crawled underneath the van to prevent it from moving, while hundreds of others surrounded it. This siege continued for eight hours, and after the local MP and the Scottish First Minister became involved in the dispute, the two men were released back into their homes.

Everyone is aghast at the reckless irresponsibility of this act – it took place in a mainly Muslim area on the very day on which Eid is celebrated, and it took place only hours after the area had been declared as the Scottish epicentre of the Indian variant Covid cases. Ironically, just before this incident unfolded, Police had been patrolling the streets, breaking up groups of more than two people, in an effort to curtail the spread.

In India the situation is worsening every day, with hundreds of bodies of Covid victims being found floating in the Ganges. Crematoria workers are running out of wood for funeral pyres, and have taken to placing the bodies of the dead into the river, instead of burning them. This is happening along the entire length of the Ganges, as villagers living along the fifteen hundred miles of its banks are also running out of fuel for funeral pyres and are, instead, placing the bodies of their loved ones into the sacred water.

In the Middle East, the war between Israel and Hamas has expanded into civil war on the streets of areas where Jewish and Palestinian Israelis have lived side by side in peace for decades. The Police in these areas have been overwhelmed by the violence, and now Israeli troops have been deployed there in an attempt to restore peace. And on the border with Gaza, Israeli troops are amassed and ready to invade.

15th May 2021

While I had been visiting Neil at the Gayathri Foundation offices, a huge group of Americans had arrived at Shanthi. I got back from the offices, had a quick bucket bath, lathered my body in *Odomos* cream, the only mosquito repellent I had found that actually worked, changed clothes, and then rushed to the temple for prayer.

The temple was mobbed, and my usual place to sit cross-legged on the floor, the back left hand corner, was taken up by a group of flush-faced white women in a variety of colourful tops and pants which tried to mimic the Indian *salwar kameez,* but didn't quite make it. There being no space left inside the Temple, I found a little stool and placed it just outside, so that I could look in and participate in the service. Being behind everyone as I was, I used this vantage point to survey the new group.

There were about thirty of them, all white, all shapes and sizes, and all ages ranging from early twenties up to mid-eighties. I say they were all white, but actually there was an Indian man amongst them. He was a beautiful - tall and slender, with an incredible head of shining silver hair cascading down his back and framing his ruggedly handsome face. I noticed that he knew all the prayers, chants, shlokas, bhajans and hymns, and said and sang them beautifully.

At supper after prayer, the new group absolutely filled the long rectangular dining hall, where we all sat cross-legged on the floor around the perimeter of the open-air space, our backs to the waist high walls, and our metal plates on the floor in front of us. The arrangement was such that everyone could see everyone else.

Four workers, each carrying a huge metal vessel filled with rice, or daal, or spiced vegetables, moved gracefully along the line of guests, dishing out the food, and pausing slightly to smile at each new guest.

We were in the habit of eating with our right hand, without the aid of cutlery, and some of the new guests didn't know what to do. Brother Joseph spotted the problem, and quickly dashed into the kitchen, returning with a plastic tub of spoons, which he went round offering to the new guests. Most of them gratefully accepted and used the utensil, but one or two brave souls imitated us, and ate with their hands.

My gaze surreptitiously scanned the newcomers as we ate in silence, and I became aware of a young Western woman whose presence simply annoyed me. For no good reason. I guessed that she was in her mid-twenties, very tall, around five feet ten inches, plumpish, and her honey blonde hair, tied into a long side plait, had a short fringe over her forehead. The fringe was about one and a half inches too short, and it looked as though she had cut it herself. To this day, I have no idea why she annoyed me, but she did. And she continued to annoy me for the next four months.

In the following days, ashram life became very strange with the presence of this large group which, although they prayed and dined with us, kept to themselves and moved around in silence, refusing to speak with anyone, as part of their spiritual practise. The Indian man could be seen speaking with the Brothers from time to time, making arrangements for group activities, and there was a definite strain between them all – a lack of warmth, and no smiles.

The group remained with us for three months, and during that time I came to discover the history of the striking Indian man and the ashram, and the reason for the uneasy tension between them and the Brothers.

17th May 2021

Annika sent me two video clips, captured by a freelance journalist, of scenes from along the banks of the Ganges. Hundreds of bodies can be clearly seen, wrapped in saffron burial robes, embedded in the sandy banks. These are the ones which were washed ashore. Yesterday it was reported that two thousand bodies were fished out from along the length of the river, using nets.

I'm glad that Annika is relatively safe staying on her family's coffee estate, in the remote hills of Karnataka.

In the early days of our friendship, shortly after we had met in Kamun, high in the hills of the south, we spent an evening together, sipping gin and the most delicious gooseberry juice made by her sister, and watching the movie, Out of Africa, starring Meryl Streep. Just as Streep's voice-over, covering the image of a freshly bloomed coffee blossom, said,

I had a farm in Africa, at the foot of the Ngong Hills ...

I turned to look at Annika, and to my amazement, her eyes, beautiful and almond shaped, the colour of dark chocolate, had filled with great big tears.

What? I asked, but she just turned away, saying nothing.

It wasn't until much later in our friendship that I came to know the whole of Annika's story, and why it was that she had come to live in Kamun, and why the sight of the coffee blossom had made her weep.

Here in Scotland, England and Wales, Lockdown has moved into Level 2 – more freedom for meeting, movement, eating and drinking in cafes, bars and restaurants. But Glasgow, Bolton and London remain in Level 3 due to the proliferation of the so-called Indian variant, and all those who took part in Friday's demonstration on the city's south side, over the arrest of the illegal immigrants, have been requested to have a test. But the Asian community in that area seem reluctant to be tested, vaccinated, or to follow the distancing guidelines. But there is poverty there, and over-crowding, and these things make it difficult for them to comply with the guidance.

Hospital admissions over the next few weeks will reveal the extent of the spread of this variant.

18th May 2021

My next visit to Neil Kavanagh of *Kavanagh's Crunchy Crisp* fame, was another whole day's adventure. We met again in his office for breakfast, which featured a typical south Indian dish called Idli Sambar, which I absolutely loved and could have eaten all day long.

The Idli part of the dish is a firm, fist-sized savoury cake, made by steaming a batter made from fermented rice, and the sambar part is a kind of thick hot and spicy soup, with lentil, onion, garlic, potato, and okra in a tomato and tamarind sauce. Idli sambar I found was not only a delicious start to the day, but it left you well satisfied until lunch time.

Over breakfast, Neil told me about his first visit to India, fifteen years previously. It had been just after his new business venture was up and running smoothly, that he decided that it was time to give himself a much-needed holiday, and as the exoticism of India, the incredible India, had fascinated him since childhood, he decided that this would be his destination. Being flush with cash and eager to splash out with his newfound fortune, he booked himself into the exclusive Delhi Oberoi Hotel to begin his exploration of the north of the country. But he only lasted in India for three days.

His face grimaced and his lips curled as he recounted the horror of what he found on the streets and backstreets and enclaves in and around the Capital – the poor, the maimed, the lepers, the ragged and torn infants begging on the streets, the amputees and the polio victims, living in filthy hovels, their broken bodies semi-covered in dirty sackcloth rags, and across the road and in his hotel, the opulence, the luxury, the excess of wealth.

The glaring disparity between the wealthy and the poor, the high caste and the low, turned his stomach and his mind, and in fear for his sanity, Neil booked the first flight home he could get.

But back in Dublin, he found that he could not get the graphic images of human misery, a misery ignored and perpetuated by those with the power to change it, out of his mind. When he closed his eyes at night to sleep, there they were – the two year' old girl whose left leg and right arm had been amputated to make her into a more appealing beggar, the many young urchins, and the elderly whose polio had condemned them a life of scuttling along the streets on all fours, like giant spiders, looking for food, the ragged lepers huddled in corners begging for Rupees. And when he eventually slept, they remained with him, peopling his dreams.

As the weeks became months, the poor, the crippled, the lame, the dispossessed, all those whose misery he had witnessed, began growing into a clamour in his mind which did not leave him day or night, and eventually their cries entered his soul. He had to return. He had to help them. Neil almost skipped over the few lines in the national newspaper which were to change his life.

A group of more than a hundred low caste Indians, Dalits, he read, are being sought by the Police and rounded up in Northern India. The story stated that this huge group had gone on a midnight rampage through a high-caste area of Patna, entering homes and waking all the men. They dragged the men from their beds and into a field where they lined them up and, one at a time, slit their throats with a machete.

Neil put the newspaper down and picked up the phone to book his flight. He was joining them in their fight for justice.

I was amazed by Neil's story, mainly because, having arrived via Sri Lanka in the south of the country, I had not yet been up north, and had not yet witnessed what he had been describing. Nor was I aware of the huge discrepancy in wealth, or of the livingness of the caste system, although I had heard about it. To me it had just been a story about life in another country, interesting, appalling, but just a story, like so many other interesting and appalling stories which make up the history of humanity, at all times and in all places.

Listening to Neil though, this particular story was beginning to become very real. I had fled Drumnock because I had found that my own life had become unbearable, but here in India, I was about to discover what unbearable really means.

20th May 2021

I was talking to Tam, the Windy Man, which means window cleaner, yesterday. He had come to collect his "windy money", the six pounds he charges for cleaning all the windows. I told him about the double murder attempts across the road.

That's nuthin, he said. Huv ye no heard aboot whit happened up in Garry Road? An' roon the Chinky's?

No, I said.

He removed the fag from between his lips and took a deep breath.

Well, he said, there wis another murder attempt *oan* the bridge at the *Chinky's*, and another *wan roon* the station, an' wait for this, he said....

Four men nabbed a man *oaf* the street, took him *tae* his *ain* flat, *pit* a pillowcase *ower* his *heid*, nail gunned him *tae* a chair, and tortured him, for six *oors*. Then they stabbed him and left him.

Oh help, I said. What's happening?

Dunno, he said. Drugs, prob'ly.

We looked at each other in silence for a while,

then Tam pocketed his six pounds, shrugged his shoulders, and left.

I sat in the living room staring out of the window, across to the field where the first stabbings had taken place. After a week of emptiness, some dog walkers had returned and were throwing balls, which were quickly retrieved and returned to them by their eagerly panting pets, and one or two toddlers were going back and forth on the swings in the play park. Life was returning to normal across the road, but the stabbings, and now torture, were continuing just around the corner, in the other direction.

I suddenly no longer felt safe living here.

21st May 2021

After Neil and I had finished breakfast, Kumar brought the vehicle, a Maruti Suzuki Gypsy, round to the office, and we climbed into the back of it. This was our first trip together to see the various projects which Gayathri had on the go. We were heading first of all to Muzum, a thirty-minute drive away, to visit the soap and jewellery-making workshops. Local women were employed there, Neil explained, and were earning enough money to keep their families healthy and well fed, and were even able to save a little.

Neil and I spent a few hours at the soap workshop in Muzum, which was really like a small factory. The women used an ancient recipe to make their soaps, a recipe which had been handed down for generations, but had then been lost after several years of extreme weather events.

There had been a heatwave, with temperatures soaring up to fifty-five degrees, followed by a drought, followed by an extraordinarily wet monsoon which caused extensive flooding and destroyed many of the villages. These weather events had devastated their homes, their crops, their cow and goat herds, and their way of life.

In the years that followed this, their main concern had been to reconstruct their dwelling places, and simply scratch enough of a living to get the food they needed to keep body and soul together. But when Neil arrived, with his *Crunchy Crisp* fortune, life had taken a turn for the better.

With Neil's money, not only were new dwelling huts constructed for the villagers, but plumbing, which supplied fresh water for drinking, cooking, toilets and washing were installed, electricity was connected, and two large buildings, which were to house the soap and jewellery-making workshops, were constructed in an area central to seven of the outlying villages.

Two of the women had eventually managed to find the old soap recipes in plastic tubs, and they had, miraculously, been preserved. The women used these old recipes, in conjunction with locally sourced dried flowers and herbs – calendula, chamomile, nettle, buckwheat, lavender, hibiscus, neem, to make the soaps. A portion of each base ingredient was put into a huge bucket, and was then covered with boiling water.

A variety of vegetable oils and secret ingredients, including goats' milk and coconut oil in some recipes, were added to the mixture, and the whole thing was then shaken vigorously in a large metal machine with various dials and knobs and settings, before being poured out to harden in a vat in the fresh air.

Once dried and hardened, a group of women, using measuring and weighing equipment, cut the soap into bars, carving a leaf or a flower into each bar before it was wrapped.

Sixty women were in full-time employment at the soap making and jewellery workshops, where they started work at ten in the morning, six days a week. Some of them, the furthest from the central hub, had to walk almost an hour to reach it, and then another hour's walk home, after they finished at four in the evening.

Their babies and infants, whom they carried to work on their backs, were tended to by six young village girls in a noisy creche, just a few hundred yards away from the workshops, and the women were free to visit them every few hours. Most of the babies and infants wore dark eyeliner and had large black kohl circles painted on their cheeks. When I enquired about them, I learned that these marks were meant to protect the children from harm, and to ward off *the Evil Eye*. When the evil spirits saw them, they believed, the ugly marks would scare them off.

These women were some of the most joyful people I have ever seen. They sang as they worked, in the most charming high-pitched piping voices, and laughed and joked and played pranks on each other like naughty schoolgirls throughout the working day. But they always managed to complete their daily quota of work, and each day a new batch of herbal soaps for all skin types and conditions were wrapped in greaseproof paper, banded round with colourful straps of paper showing pictures of the flowers and herbs in the recipe, the name of the soap, and the skin conditions they were good for.

The soaps were then boxed and sealed and collected by a small battered old van which took them to the Post Office in Kalitooly, from whence they were sent on to their final destinations – the upmarket shops in Chennai and Pondicherry, Bombay and Delhi, Hampi and Rishikesh, and all over India. And to keep Neil happy, batches of the soaps were also sent to the top Body Emporium in Grafton Street, Dublin, where the soaps were sold for four Euros a bar, and were extremely popular.

24th May 2021

I returned to Shanthi at around four in the afternoon, after an exhilarating day out with Neil. The delicious aromatic scents of the various soaps lingered on in my nostrils, making me quite pleasantly heady and light-hearted, and I was still wearing the colourfully jingling bangles and bracelets and neckpiece which two of the women from the jewellery workshop had given me as I was leaving.

The women had all gathered round while the gifts were presented, and as the two women placed the bangles on my arms and the neckpiece around my neck, delicately moving my long loose hair out of the way, all the others were laughing, smiling, chattering in delight at the sight of this blonde-haired, blue-eyed white woman, being adorned with *their* jewellery. I loved their high-pitched piping voices and the joy of their being, and as I left them and their workshops, I felt lifted by them and by the time spent in their company.

When I got to Shanthi I had hoped to have a quick bucket bath and make it in time for the four o'clock talk. But when I reached the ashram, the heavy air of gloom there was a palpable antithesis to the day I'd just had, and I immediately felt both concerned and confused.

Instead of the guests chattering and drinking tea

in the circle, they were all just sitting there, grim-faced and silent, and making no move to finish off their drinks or to head for the meditation hall. Perplexed, I walked slowly to the circle and sat down on the wall beside Alan.

What's happened? I asked him.

Well, he said, there's no talk today for one thing. Brother Joseph and the others have gone to Petapatalli.

Petapatalli was the next village to ours, about three miles along the road.

There's been an incident, he said, a serious one, or so we were told. Brother Joseph was in a state when he left on his moped. I've never seen him looking like that – his face was contorted with shock or something as he left. And then the other Brothers, Yesudas, Kumaresan, Peter, James, they all left in the jeep shortly after he did. They all looked grim, shocked. That was about two hours ago, and no word from them since.

Oh God, I said. I wonder what could have happened.

I left the circle for my hut, where I bucket-bathed, combed my hair, put on a little lipstick, and climbed over the fence to the Sadhu's hut, where I found him sitting in silence on the wooden bench on his porch.

We looked at each and began laughing. That's the way our meetings always began, with deep chuckling laughter and joy. I sat down beside him, and we stayed like that, in silence, for some time, and then I recounted the day I'd just had, ending the storytelling with an account of the atmosphere just across the fence, in the ashram. His eyes widened. But he made no comment.

He brewed us some chai, getting the water into the pot directly from the little hand pump just beside the porch, heating it on top of the small gas stove before adding the powdered chai mix, some sugar and some cardamom and vanilla pods. We sipped the brew in silence, and then moved inside the hut to continue with the lessons on *pranayama* and *vipassana* meditation, the most difficult and radical meditation practise in the world.

The Sadhu was an excellent teacher – I knew this from my own years as a teacher and my own understanding, that, in order to teach someone, you must meet them exactly where they are, and then lead them forward, step by step, developing their own inherent abilities along the way, to a new level of understanding. And this is what he did with me.

He began by teaching me *pranayama* as an exercise in alternate nostril breathing, showing me how to hold my hand, arranging the fingers in such a way that the thumb was held down while the fingers were left free to first obstruct one nostril, and then the other.

The thumb is held down, he explained, because it is dominant and it represents the ego, and all of our practices are designed to weaken the grip of the ego and conditioned mind over the pure untainted mind, which is the gateway to our true identity. And this is what we seek, because this is what we have lost our connection to. Our true identity, and our true nature.

It was a new concept to me, this idea of a doubleness of identity. I thought I knew who I was, more or less, and would have summarised it primarily as a lover of

Christ, and then something along the lines of my name, place of birth, family, genetic predispositions, the time I was born into, my religion and beliefs, where I was educated and worked, what I liked and disliked, my opinions and attitudes, what I loved, and what I hated, my hopes and dreams, what I sought in order to make me happy.

All those things, I would have said back then, were what made up my identity.

But no, the Sadhu told me, all those things represent who you *are not*, and as you continuously identify with them, they keep you trapped in your false identity, your false self. But you love Christ, he said, as I also do, and that will make the journey much easier.

We will continue to work together, he said, until you begin to catch glimpses of your true identity. And the *pranayama* and the meditation are our tools.

I left the Sadhu in the forest and arrived in the Temple ten minutes early, making sure that I got my usual place to sit cross-legged on the floor at the back left-hand corner – my safe place, where I could see everyone, but only a few could see me. It was already filling up with the silent pale-faced Americans, but I got my place and settled down, carefully arranging my long white dress designed by me and stitched by James the tailor, over my feet and ankles, and my dupatta, an eight-foot-long shawl, over my arms and hands.

Although I always covered myself in *Odomos* cream at mosquito feeding times – dawn and dusk – there were always one or two who made it through the barrier to make a hole and suck some blood. Intermittent loud slaps were heard throughout morning and evening prayer, as blood thirsty mosquitoes were swatted from naked arms and ankles.

We waited until ten minutes after seven for the Brothers to arrive, and then the whispering within the congregation began. There were two young Brothers there, novices from a neighbouring ashram. They whispered to each other, and then they nervously began the prayer service. It was a clumsy affair, but we managed to make our way through it and afterwards to the dining hall, where we ate in a gloomy silence, and then returned to our huts.

By the following morning the Brothers had returned, and the daily schedule resumed as normal, albeit heavily, and in silence.

As no-one had told us what had happened in Petapatalli, rumours began circulating, firstly that there had been a rape of one of the young village women while she had been out toileting in the forest, and then that an enraged bull had gored some young men to death, and then that a crazed madman had gone on the rampage with a machete. Eventually these rumours began to reach the ears of Brother Joseph, and he summoned all the guests to the meditation hall immediately after lunch.

He looked ghastly as he sat down, arranging his white dhoti carefully as he gracefully sank into the lotus position and faced us.

Let us pray, he said, and lowered his head.

We all did likewise, closing our eyes and bowing our heads.

There has been a tragic accident in Petapatalli, he

said, looking up. A young man and a young woman, still in their teens.

A tragic accident, he repeated.

A bullock cart, with two heavy horned bullocks was left untethered when the sound of a vehicle backfiring startled them. They charged around the streets of the village, still harnessed to the cart, in a frenzy, and when they trampled the two villagers in their path, they left them dead.

The Brothers and I have been with their families all night, cleaning the bodies, doing puja, and preparing them for cremation. We are now returning to the village to attend their funerals and offer comfort to their families.

Please keep them all in your prayers.

With that, he stood up and walked past us and out of the meditation hall. We didn't see him again until the following day, when everything appeared to return to normal.

The next morning I overslept, missing the five o'clock *Nama Japa*, the six thirty Mass, and breakfast. I say 'overslept', but, in truth, this had become a habitual pattern for me – since my first two weeks at Shanthi, I had never gone for the five o'clock *Nama Japa* or the morning prayers, or for breakfast.

My habit had become to wake up at around eight o'clock, which was vegetable chopping time, put on the little stove to heat some water, dress quickly and, with a large metal tumbler in hand, make my way to the cowsheds where Prashant, the cowman, would be busily milking.

I would hold the tumbler to whichever teat he happened to be pulling on, and he would shift the angle of the teat, squirting the milk directly into the tumbler. The warm frothing milk made a whooshing sound as it hit the bottom of the metal cup, and its smell was warm and delicious. Sometimes the cow would look back at me with her docile eyes to see what was happening with her udder, her milk.

Then I would go back to my hut and stare into space as I drank the milky coffee. Only after that did I venture out to the central dining area, past the vegetable chopping guests, and into the kitchen proper to find Julie and Papita, and sit down on the floor to have breakfast with them. No-one seemed to mind this odd behaviour of mine, and Brother Joseph, who knew that I was often awake into the early hours of the morning painting, approved of it. So no-one else could complain.

After breakfast with Julie and Papita, I would collect all the vegetable peelings and take them to the little field beside the cow sheds where the new calves were kept, and feed them the treats.

But at around seven thirty that morning, I was awakened by a loud banging on the door, and a voice which I recognised as Kumar's shouting,

Manee Madam, Manee Madam, please wake up.

I opened the door a crack, and saw Kumar's bright-eyed face looking concerned and harried.

Manee Madam, he said, Neil Sir has sent me.

He cannot be meeting with you this morning,

Manee Madam. He to Petapatalli go. Terrible things, *rumba* terrible things, happening in Petapatalli, and Neil Sir, he must go.

He will come for you after the lunch, he said. He will take you to the office. Two o'clock Manee Madam, he said, and then rushed off.

The plan had been to meet up at the Gayathri Foundation in the village at ten o'clock, and then make the forty-minute drive to the training organic farm in Muzum. We had planned to have a tour of the place and then sit in on one of the organic farming lessons which were regularly given to the local subsistence farmers, and finish off by having a lunch made only from the training farm's produce.

So, after coffee and breakfast and feeding the calves, I settled down on the veranda for an unexpected morning of painting in the sunshine and shade of the banyan tree.

I was working on what was my sixth painting since arriving at Shanthi, and the work was as yet a mystery of greens and blues, with wavering fronds and the suggestion of a blossom, pushing upwards towards the light; there was a watery feeling to the whole thing, and it felt as though something underneath the sea was struggling to breathe, to burst the bud and grow up out of the water, into the light of day. It was a dynamic piece, and I was completely absorbed in it.

I missed the ten o'clock break at the tea circle to keep painting, but made a mug of coffee in the hut using the leftover milk from morning, heated over the small gas stove. There was a gentle cooling breeze coming in over the river, and birdsong from the forest. I was lost in the sounds and sensations, the colours and forms emerging from my fingertips, and I almost jumped out of my skin when Milly, a new friend from Ohio, suddenly appeared through a clearing in the trees and caught sight of me in my other world.

Oh, goodness Milly, you didn't half give me a fright, I laughed, beckoning her onto the veranda.

Two other women arrived just behind her, two of the silent Americans, and all four of us sat around on the veranda, while Milly did the introductions. Her companions were Priscilla and Wendy, both from California, and both with the study group.

We had to break our silence, they giggled. We were going mad!

We all laughed heartily, and Priscilla and Wendy continued laughing so vigorously that Milly and I had to join in again. Eventually we all stopped for air, and to come back down to earth.

Milly has told us that you're an artist, said Wendy. May we have a look at your work?

Of course, I said, jumping up and into the hut and out again, a makeshift portfolio in hand.

I spread the paintings out on the veranda, and we all gathered round to look at them.

27th May 2021

Black fungus. That's the new horror story coming out of India.

A pleasant doctor from Andhra Pradesh yesterday told Sky News viewers that a number of patients who have recently recovered from the new strain of Covid have complained of nose and throat problems and, upon examination, it has been found that a black fungus, known as *murcomycosis*, is the culprit.

It's a rare fungus, Doctor Sanjay explained, and a very dangerous one, a very aggressive one. It affects mainly the nose and the eyes, but sometimes the brain, and around half of those who become infected, die of it. We are being kept very busy these days, he went on, carrying out the three hour' long operations needed to remove the eyeballs in severely infected patients. This is to stop the growth of the fungus, and prevent it from reaching the brain.

Oh God.

This is truly apocalyptic.

On a brighter note, it seems that the Pfizer and Astra Zeneca vaccines do indeed provide a measure of protection from the new variant, but only after both doses have been given. Pfizer gives ninety percent protection, Astra Zeneca sixty percent. I'm Astra Zeneca. And only one dose so far. And it's spreading quickly in Glasgow.

I was telling Molly about all the stabbings around here, and was shocked when she told me that around three hundred members of Glasgow's two biggest crime families live in and around Drumknock, and that they've gone to war over drugs.

How do you know? I asked her.

Molly explained that ever since Stuart, her godson, in a fit of madness in his late teens, had briefly joined one of the gangs, she had always kept an eye on what they were up to.

We both marvelled for a while that her lovely godson had briefly entered into that dark world of drug and crime, and then emerged again, apparently unscathed, and was now happily married with three bouncing baby boys. Stuart had got over it, but Molly never had.

I feel scared, I told Molly. It's all just a bit too close.

Don't be scared, she replied. They're only interested in killing each other.

Cold comfort.

28th May 2021

Yesterday in Britain an enquiry into the Government's handling of the pandemic in its early days began when Dominic Cummings, Boris Johnson's then righthand man and Chief Advisor, now arch enemy, carried out a verbal massacre of the Prime Minister and Matt Hancock, the Health Secretary.

For seven hours he poured scorn on them as being incompetent, self-serving buffoons, who lied incessantly, to both colleagues and the public, and, he said, their decision-making and actions had caused massive harm to the people of Britain.

He claimed that Johnson had initially believed the virus to be harmless, and at one point toyed with the idea of having the country's leading virologist, Professor Chris Whitty, inject him with it, live on television, to show the public that there was nothing to worry about. He also claimed that, later on, when it had become clear that the virus was a problem, Johnson had refused to lockdown the country, saying that it would only be eighty-year-olds who would die.

But the most damning evidence of all was his claim, which has since proven to be true, that they gave the go ahead for elderly people to be discharged from hospitals directly into care homes, without being tested. They thereby caused a massive spread of the virus in the homes, and tens of thousands of unnecessary deaths.

Sic a parcel o' rogues, as our very own Rabbie Burns said way back in 1791, Sic a parcel o' rogues.

29th May 2021

Bang on the dot of two o'clock, Kumar rolled up in the Gypsy to take me across the road to the Gayathri offices. When we arrived, Neil was standing over the gas stove, adding the final ingredients to what he had dubbed as 'the finest Irish chai in all of India', and it definitely did have something in it which gave it a not too unpleasant kick. Its aroma and taste were quite different to the Sadhu's brew, and drinking it sometimes left me giggly. After my first tumbler of it a few weeks previously, I had surreptitiously glanced around the room to see if there happened to be a bottle of Jamieson's stuffed in a corner.

Neil looked up from the steaming pot as I entered. I immediately noticed that his face was unusually serious as he greeted me. But still, he took both my hands in his and kissing me once on each cheek, he sang,

Good day to you Marney of the pale blue eyes, to the tune of a favourite Irish love song, and he beckoned me to a seat.

He continued humming the tune gently to himself, a tune which I knew by heart and loved well, *The Mountains of Mourne*, as he completed the brew and poured it into two metal tumblers, and then sat down beside me.

There are some things I need to tell you about Marney, he said, pulling up a chair beside mine and putting his tumbler on the table. Kumar's head appeared around the door to ask if madam would like some laddus to sweeten her chai and, of course, she did.

Did you hear about what happened in Petapatalli Marney? Neil asked, becoming sombre.

Yes, I replied. What a dreadful accident. And how awful for their poor parents.

It was no accident, Neil said, no accident at all.

My jaw dropped. What do you mean? I asked.

You've heard about the caste system, right?

Yes, I nodded.

Well, he said, what happened in our neighbours' village on Thursday happened as a result of this hideous system. The dead girl and boy, Bhavna and Babul, had fallen in love and wanted to marry, but because they each belonged to a different sub-caste, their marriage was forbidden.

What is a sub-caste? I asked.

Fingering his goatee thoughtfully, Neil looked to the side for a moment before continuing.

Okay, he said, you know that there are four main Castes, right? The top are the Brahmins, and they're known as the priestly caste, then come the Kshatriyas, the warrior caste, then the Vaishyas, which is a kind of business and agricultural class, and at the bottom are the Shudras, the labouring and serving caste. And the untouchables, or Dalits, God help them, are on the bottom rung of the Shudras.

It's a hierarchical system, and the caste you're born into determines your social status and standing for life. It sounds quite simple, he said, but there's a catch. Within these four main castes there are, quite literally, thousands of sub-divisions, and again, these are all ranked in order of the hierarchy, and let me tell you, he said, these villagers cling to their caste and sub-caste and live it religiously.

Kumar reappeared around the door and placed a metal platter of bright orange sticky laddus, a sweet treat made from sugar, ghee, flour, and garnished with chopped nuts and dried raisins, on the table beside us.

So poor Bhavna and Babul from Petapatalli, Neil went on, after they'd asked and been denied permission to marry, eloped to Delhi one night and were married there in secret. They managed to find simple accommodation and basic jobs, he as a daily labourer and she as a maid, and that is how they began their married life.

After they'd been there for six months, Bhavna, the girl, began missing her mother, and eventually she sent her message, telling her the story of her love for Babul, how she could not live without him, and how they had been married and were now settled.

Her mother, Kalki, received the message and quickly shared it with her husband Raju, and then with the parents of Babul who lived close by. The four parents met and discussed the situation they found themselves in, and together they sent a message back to Bhavna, pleading with her to return to Petapatalli with Babul.

They were forgiven, her mother told her, and

could return home to live out their lives beside their friends and family. Everyone's heart was breaking, she said, because they were no longer with them.

When Bhavna and Babul received this message from Kalki, they were over-joyed. They immediately sent her a message saying that they were booked on the next train to Kalitooli, and would be with them within a few days.

When they arrived back in Petapatalli, there was a gang waiting for them.

Within an hour they had been punched and kicked and beaten to a pulp with heavy sticks and clubs and battered with stones, and eventually their lifeless bodies were dragged around the dusty streets of Petapatalli, before being left lying in the tiny village square for all to see.

As I listened to Neil, I could feel myself falling deeper and deeper into a kind of shocked silence. It was completely beyond comprehension, this tale he was telling me, and my brain just couldn't't compute it. But I wanted to hear more.

Well, Marney, said Neil, that's the sorry tale of what happened to Bhavna and Babul. There was no bullock cart, no vehicle backfiring and no startled bullocks charging around. It was a double premeditated murder, carried out by an entire village. So put that in your pipe and smoke it, he said.

But what about the law, I said. Surely the Police must have become involved after these crazy deaths of two really young people?

Oh yes, he said, they did.

He adjusted himself in his chair and gazed downwards for a while.

After the bodies had lain out for two hours, he said, the Police were called. When they arrived in the form of Santosh and Shantanu from Anapati, the next village down river, they showed them the bodies. By then they had been removed indoors for washing and puja and prayer. Tearfully, and with loud-pitched wailing, Kalki told them the terrible story, that Bhavna and Babul had just returned from the big city, the Capital of the country, in their happily married state, when disaster struck. And that's what they wrote in their report, although they knew the truth of what had happened.

You can't underestimate the power and hold which the caste system has over everyone in India, from the highest to the lowest – they all honour it, and they all uphold it. Even the Untouchables accept it – they honour it as their role, as their rightful destiny. And so it goes on, ineluctable, self-perpetuated, intractable.

Help me fight it Marney, Neil said. Help me fight it. We can never overcome it, but we can help to ease some of the suffering which it engenders.

I was speechless, tear-blown and ravaged as I staggered back across the road to Shanthi to find the sanctuary of my hut and the comfort of the wooden cot. As the tears streamed down my face, the words of Seamus Heaney's elemental poem, *Punishment,* began resounding in my mind. Over and over again his refrain, his understanding, and his guilt over his knowledge and understanding of the intimate revenge of the tribe on those who transgress

its boundaries. He wrote,
I can feel the tug
of the halter at the nape
of her neck, the wind
on her naked front.

It blows her nipples
to amber beads,
it shakes the frail rigging
of her ribs.
...
Little adulteress,
before they punished you
you were flaxen-haired,
undernourished, and your
tar-black face was beautiful.
My poor scapegoat,

I almost love you
but would have cast, I know,
the stones of silence.
I am the artful voyeur

of your brain's exposed
and darkened combs,

your muscles' webbing
and all your numbered bones:

I who have stood dumb
when your betraying sisters,
cauled in tar,
wept by the railings,

who would connive
in civilized outrage
yet understand the exact
and tribal, intimate revenge.

The poem, the words, the poet's pondering of a body preserved in peat and dug up after two thousand years, the recollection of old Germany and old Ireland's form of tribal revenge for those who broke its rules, was a perfect fit for the fate of Bhavna and Babul, and just as I was sinking deeper into a kind of numb and hopeless helplessness, my eyes fell upon a pattern on the thin mat covering the bed.

There it was again. The symbol of the three concentric circles, tiny, hand-stitched, and tucked into the top right-hand corner of the mat. It felt like a sign, a message from beyond, that I was not alone, that I was exactly where I needed to be.

31st May 2021

In the days that followed my visit with Neil, I remained in a kind of stunned silence, barely leaving my hut, except for one meal per day at lunchtime, and a walk around the ashram's beautiful flower-fringed paths. I had become like one of the pale-faced silent Americans I saw each day.

Neil sent Kumar to bring me across the road, but I declined, saying that I needed some time just to be alone, for prayer, meditation, reflection. I said I would come over in the next week or so, and reluctantly, Kumar accepted this.

Brother Joseph noticed the shift in my demeanour and my absence from prayer and meals, and he invited me to the meditation hall for spiritual guidance and meditation practise. I accepted the meditation practise but said that I'd prefer to remain in silence. I had been sworn to secrecy over the story of Bhavna and Babul, and as the Brothers had been told the cover story of the bullock cart accident, I could not discuss the matter, even with Brother Joseph.

We met in the meditation hall an hour before midday prayer, and Brother Joseph beckoned me to sit cross-legged on a mat on the floor facing him. He was the darkest man I had ever seen, a brown so deep that it was almost jet, and on his handsome rugged face he wore a little moustache and a box beard, typical of the men in the area. His eyes were of a deep burnt umber and the whites of them shone like the sun. He was tall and strong, around six feet tall, and well built.

Many's the time, as I sat on the veranda in the dark of an evening painting in the glow of the lamp, I would look up and be startled at the sight of a headless man walking by. No matter how many times it happened, I would jump up and shriek at the sight, only moments later to realise that it was Brother Joseph, draped in his flowing white robes, walking by, the darkness of his face and head blending perfectly into the night's hue, and giving the impression that he had no head at all.

This jump and shriek never startled him though, and immediately after shrieking, I would see a pair of flashing eyes and brilliant teeth, and would feel foolish and blush.

During my weeks in the ashram, I had developed an immense sense of respect for this man, as I witnessed his tireless work and dedication to God, and his spiritual community, and to the poor in the villages. I drank deeply of the wisdom he imparted during his talks, and I had become aware of his deep humility, his selflessness, and his maturity in the face of the antics of often silly guests, myself amongst them, and the occasional disputes amongst the Brothers. I felt that he, singlehandedly, kept the ashram going smoothly. He was both the heart of the place and its spirit, as well as its backbone.

As we sat facing one another, relaxed and comfortable, he began talking me through a meditation practice which I had not experienced before.

Close your eyes, he began, and be still.

Open up your ears, he continued, and listen to all the faraway sounds, the sounds of the traffic coming from the main road, the swish of the vehicles, the beeping of horns and the screech of brakes, the barking of the dogs, the sounds of the cows far off in the distance...

Now come closer, and listen to the sounds near to us, the rustle of the fallen leaves in the breeze outside the window, the sounds of the peacocks pecking for food, the song of the birds, the wind in the trees, the sound of your breath...

Now bring your attention, your awareness to the tips of your toes, resting on them for only a moment, and moving on to the soles of your feet, the tops of your feet, your ankles and calves and shins and knees. Just allow your awareness to rest for a moment on each part and then move on without hesitating; if there is pain, notice it and move on, if there is tension, notice it and move on, if there is sensation, notice it and move on ...

He continued guiding me through this body scan, going from the tips of my toes to the top of my head, and then directing my attention to the breath, the in-breath and its sensations in the nostrils and as it entered the body, and the out-breath, and its sensations.

We lingered on the breath, which felt like a calm and gently swaying sea, for a few moments and then moved on.

Bring your attention to the space between your eyebrows, he said, and gently, softly, focus your eyes there. Imagine the vast blue endless expanse of the sky before you, around you, within you. Notice any thoughts which appear in your mind, and then let them dissolve like clouds in the warmth of the sun.

Just allow the thoughts to appear, linger a moment, and pass away, without attachment to them, without engaging with them, but just noticing them, and allowing them to pass away as your mind expands into the vast blue sky, rising above the turbulence of the clouds, and resting in the space above them, facing the brilliance of the sun.

Rest here in the vastness of the sky, the brilliance of the sun, just allowing the clouds to appear, move through the space, and disappear...

We sat together in this vast and brilliant space for a long time, swaying gently back and forth with each in breath and each exhalation, moving deeper and deeper into silence, expanding more and more into this infinite space which rested just behind our closed eyes.

After some time, Brother Joseph again spoke, drawing my attention back again to the breath, to the body, to the sounds both near and far, and eventually, through the opening of my eyes, back into the meditation hall.

He then rose from the lotus position and silently left the room.

6th June 2021

It's a gorgeous summer's day here in Drumnock. I'm sitting in the living room drinking my usual brew of dark Mayan coffee, marked five in terms of strength, infused with creamy milk. I can see out through the window to the trees, now thick with their summer blankets of green in all its glorious shades, from the darkest of sap greens through the brilliance of emerald to the sparkle of Chartreuse in the new growth.

Beyond the trees I can see the field. The Police are there, five of them, and they are cordoning off a large area with tape. They have two cars and one large white van. There are no children swinging in the play park, and no dog walkers.

Tam the Windy Man called by yesterday.

There's another area, he told me, just beyond the bushes which fringe the field. It's on the canal bank side, he said, and this is now being cordoned off.

And in the Glasgow Evening Times, I read that another gangland war has broken out, this time in Edinburgh, and yesterday three men were admitted to the city's Royal Infirmary in critical conditions after being attacked by a gang who slashed into their necks and heads with machetes.

On the pandemic front, the Indian variant, now renamed Delta to avoid stigmatising the British Indian community, is spreading like wildfire. Around eighty percent of the spiking new cases here are Delta. But thankfully, hospital admissions and deaths remain low, giving us reassurance that the vaccination programme is being successful.

More than half of the adult population have now received both doses.

8th June 2021

A few days after the meditation with Brother Joseph, he came to my hut and suggested that it was time for me to move to a different hut, one in a more secluded location where I would not be disturbed by passers-by, and where I could deepen in meditation practise.

It took just over an hour to move all my belongings from the first hut, underneath the banyan tree, to the second hut, which was situated on the outer edge of the ashram, overlooking the paddy field and beyond that, into the eucalyptus forest, and beyond that still further, the sacred river.

There was an opening in the forest directly facing the new hut, and on Sundays the young boys from the village played cricket here. The boys had nothing but joy, and as they played in their ragged clothes with sticks and stones for bats and balls, their shrieks and cheers and shouts were marvellous.

It wasn't until the third day in the new hut that I came to realise that just off to the side of a clearing, a hundred yards or so to the right, lay the cremation ground for the village. Shortly after sunrise on that day I was awakened by the smell of smoke and burning, and when

I opened the door to look and see, I saw beside the cricket ground a raging fire, surrounded by village men.

Many times I had seen the molten embers and ash of burnt-out funeral pyres on my daily walks into town, but had never seen one ablaze like this. I was stilled and humbled by the sight and by the enormity of the occasion, and sat down on the veranda to pray along with the mourners.

The following morning, I again sat out on the veranda, gazing across the paddy field, hypnotised by its swaying back and forth like an enormous ocean of green. By and by a villager came walking, carrying a machete in his right hand, and moving towards the now burnt-out funeral pyre.

I watched as he used a long stick to rummage around in the ashen debris, and then, when he found the skull of the deceased, how he raised the machete above his head, and how he brought it crashing down into the skull, smashing it over and over and over again, until it was broken. And in this way, he released the spirit of his father, and freed it to fly to God.

9th June 2021

I saw Molly yesterday for the first time in almost a year. It had been our habit to meet every couple of weeks for lunch in the West End, and to talk.

We have known each other since we were girls, and yesterday, after an outdoor lunch in the Botanical Gardens Tearoom, we retraced the steps of our friendship back through the gardens, with their luminous blossoming hydrangea in a symphony of pinks and whites, and the soft yellow summer magnolia, all in full bloom, back out through the gilded metal gates of the park, and onto the Great Western Road.

A few blocks west along the road, we came to the terrace of magnificent Georgian townhouses where we had first met. We were two of the five secretaries in the Department of Child and Family Psychiatry, and the whole department had been decanted to one of these gorgeous townhouses whilst renovation works were carried out in the Glasgow Children's Hospital.

The long row of houses was set back from the Great Western Road in a curving terrace, fringed and sheltered from the road by huge mature evergreen trees. It was onto these very trees that our gaze would fall during our long intense religious and philosophical conversations, which left the three other secretaries in our office fascinated and spellbound.

Molly had been raised in the Plymouth Brethren sect, and I in the Catholic Church, as an Irish Catholic within an Irish Catholic family. We were both open-minded and intense in our love for Christ, and the differences in our upbringings and conditioned minds gave us an endless supply of fuel for deep conversations about God. Many decades later, these conversations continue, unabated in passion and intensity.

It was a great nourishment for my soul to spend time with Molly again, now that we are both doubly vaccinated against the virus, and now that outdoor dining is allowed. We could reach out and touch one another, and we could hug. Two weary old travellers, walking, and sometimes limping, along the often harsh and rocky road towards our forever home.

10th June 2021

The sights and sounds surrounding my new hut and its location on the outer edge of Shanthi provided me with a fresh and different experience of the ashram.

In the early mornings, I would be gently awakened by the sounds coming from the large outdoor meditation hall, the original one which had been built during Brother Magnus's time. Unlike the new octagonal building, which was fully enclosed from the elements by strong pillars which supported its seven large windows, all with mosquito netting, the old one was fully open from waist height so that the birds could flit in and out through the space, or a breeze from the river could come and cool you as you sat.

It was perfectly circular and made of concrete, painted over with heavy duty industrial paint, maroon in colour. It had an outer rim, like a veranda, and three steps down to the ground. There was a two feet high wall enclosing the meditation space, and right in the centre of the space there was a sculpture of Christ.

It was a fascinating piece of artwork. Joined as one in the centre, the sculpture showed three faces of Christ, all identical and all facing outwards in different directions. They all sat in the lotus position, garlanded with flowers, and dressed in the loincloth of the Sannyasin. It was an arresting image, and one which forced the viewer to apprehend both the mystery of the Trinity and the inner journey of the Sannyasin, and to somehow grapple to comprehend the connection between these two disparate and apparently unconnected spiritual truths from two very different religious traditions.

The sculpture somehow summed up in visual form the truth which Brother Magnus had struggled to communicate to the world during the last forty years of his life, the truth that at the centre and when boiled down to absolute essences, these two religious traditions point to the same invisible Truth – that God is One, and that we are not separated from God in our deepest core.

The old meditation hall was around one hundred and fifty yards to the left of my new hut, and aligned with it, and these were the only two buildings on this edge of the ashram.

During their three month' stay with us, the American group had taken over the use of this hall, which otherwise lay unused, almost abandoned, except by the exotic birds which sometimes nested there, and of course, the snakes, which sometimes slithered into its shade during the heat of the day.

The Americans had come to Shanthi for a spiritual retreat focussing on yoga and meditation, and to deepen their knowledge of the philosophy of the chakra system, and to engage in chakra meditations. Their leader and teacher was this ruggedly handsome Indian man with the incredible head of shining silver hair, whose name I had learned was Prakash.

It was their habit and practise to make their way,

in a meditative walk, from their huts to the hall just before dawn each day, and find a spot to sit in silence until the sun's rays began percolating through the light and shade and movement of the trees, landing in glimmering spots here and there on the floor of the hall, and illuminating shafts of dusty space in the air. At this point, Prakash would begin the day's practises with the ancient and most revered of chants, the Gayathri Mantra. My mind was now daily aroused from its slumber by the sound of thirty voices, some sure and certain, others hesitant and slow.

*Om bhur bhuvah swah*a
Tat savitur varenyam
Bhargo devasya dheemahi
Dhiyo yonah prachodayat

These four lines, whose meaning is,

We meditate on the glory of the Creator
Who has created the universe
Who is worthy of worship
Who is the embodiment of all knowledge and light
Who is the remover of all sin and ignorance

are repeated one hundred and eight times, reflecting the vision of the Vedic mathematicians, who saw this number as representing the wholeness of the sun, moon and earth and the complete presence of God within them, and within the space which contains them.

This chant, which opened their day, took around

forty-five minutes to complete, and after it there always followed a period of rich and vibrating silence before Prakash began to speak.

Although I was close to the hall and the chanting was easy to hear, Prakash's voice was quiet, and I could not make out the words which he spoke, and the end of the chant was always my cue to get up from the cot, put on a pot of water to heat on the stove, and make my way down to find Prashant in the cow sheds for my warm morning milk, squooshed directly from the udder and into the tumbler, frothing up into what would become the best cappuccino in the world.

After their morning session, the Americans would make their way silently from the hall, their footsteps rustling the fallen leaves which lay on the ground behind my hut as they passed, and down to the dining room for breakfast. One morning one of the Americans chose a different path down through the trees to breakfast, a path which led her directly in front of my hut, where I sat on a rocking chair sipping the delicious coffee and gazing out over the paddy to the forest and the river.

She looked startled when she saw me, and something hard and sharp flashed in her eyes.

I smiled at her, but she did not return my smile. I recognised her as the young woman whose presence had annoyed me in the dining hall, the young woman whose fringe was around one and a half inches too short. I supposed that she had cut it herself. I didn't like her and, as I was to come to realise during the days ahead, this feeling was very much mutual. We, each of us, seemed to be projecting something of our own hidden darkness out of ourselves, and onto the other.

11th June 2021

One morning in Shanthi I arrived for breakfast with Julie and Papita, just as the regular guests were busily chopping the vegetables for lunch and supper – mounds of carrots, onions, garlic, okra, yumyums, and beets were being quickly sliced and diced and poured into metal basins, their peels discarded to the plastic bucket by the side of the chopping table. Milly laughed and smiled as I passed them, calling me a lazy sod, and asking me when her painting would be ready.

Soon, I said. Very soon.

The other guests were intrigued, and as they began asking Milly about this painting, I noticed out of the corner of my eye an altercation taking place between Brother Yesudas and Prakash over in the tea circle. They were too far away for me to hear what they were saying, and as they spoke in Tamil I would not have understood anyway, but their body language, their angry tones, their wild gesticulations, and the rising purple in their faces all bespoke of trouble.

I had noticed the previous evening during prayer that one of the Americans, an older lady, perhaps in her early eighties, who always stayed close to Prakash, had been singing out quite loudly, and, because of her deafness, she was often out of time with the hymns and chants. Her disruption of the flow of the music had drawn the baleful attention of Brother Yesudas, the ashram's musical maestro, and over and over again he turned his head to flash her a scornful glance of warning to stop it.

But her eyesight was also poor, and so she remained loud, out of time and unaware, and I struggled to stop myself from giggling out loud.

Yesudas was a stunningly handsome man, tall and slender with long shining black ringlets framing his delicate face. He carried within himself an air of confidence and had a certain refinement of feature, both of which gave him an aristocratic air. He played the sitar and sang and chanted like an angel. He was the charming star of the ashram, and most of the visitors, the foreign women, and some of the men, fell immediately in love him – his dazzling good looks, his magical music, his mellifluous voice. But like many artists, he had a quicksilver temperament, and could sometimes seem arrogant and haughty, looking down his long, elegant nose at those who annoyed him, including myself, in my moments of silliness.

And I could see that this morning Yesudas's ire had begun to overflow onto the gentleness of Prakash, and I wondered briefly if it was because of the deaf American and her out of time singing.

After breakfast I walked into town, the first time I had done so since hearing of the deaths of Bhavna and Babul. My mind had been disturbed by the story of their deaths, and it had plunged me into an inner exploration of all the times and places all over the world where this practise of honour killing had and continues to take place.

I wondered at the power of the different societal groups and how much of their lives, of all our lives, were dominated by their conditioned minds and their adherence to shared beliefs about themselves, their families, their place in the world and most of all, their identities.

The incomprehensible hold these beliefs held over everyone had, throughout history, caused war and its attendant culture of rape and torture and theft between groups of people, and given rise to the harsh reality of tribal punishments, mutilations, and death within them.

It was not confined to India. It was endemic in the human race itself, and the mesmerising poetry of Seamus Heaney, who had realised the truth of this disturbing phenomenon decades before I had, had been softly playing itself over and over again in the background of all that I had done since the deaths of the young couple. He had witnessed it directly in his home country of Ireland, and had then learned of how it had been going on since the dawn of humanity, as far back as we could see.

For him, the bodies of victims perfectly preserved in the peat bogs of Europe and brought back to the light of day through archaeological digs had become the immortalised and sacralised emblems of some of the darkness in our world.

The Tollund Man, a poem in three parts describing Heaney's response to the exhumation of a corpse sacrificed to strange gods more than two and half thousand years ago, and dug up in Jutland in 1950, seemed to me to encapsulate something of the savagery in the human soul, and the barbarity of its expressions.

Some day I will go to Aarhus, he *wrote,*

To see his peat-brown head,

The mild pods of his eyelids,

His pointed skin cap...

Naked except for

The cap, noose and girdle,
I will stand a long time...

I could risk blasphemy,
Consecrate the cauldron bog
Our holy ground and pray
Him make germinate
The scattered, ambushed
Flesh of labourers, Stockinged corpses
Laid out in the farmyards,

Tell-tale skin and teeth
Flecking the sleepers
Of four young brothers,
Trailed for miles along the lines.

Something of his sad freedom
As he rode the tumbril
Should come to me, driving,
Saying the names,
Tollund, Grauballe, Nebelgard,

Watching the pointing hands
Of country people,

Not knowing their tongue.

Out here in Jutland
In the old man-killing parishes
I will feel lost,
Unhappy and at home.

Lost, unhappy and at home. That last line of Heaney's poem stayed with me as I walked through the forest, the thorns of the path scratching at my ankles and tearing at the hems of my dress as I moved along the banks of the dried riverbed.

Some village women were out scavenging for fallen twigs and branches to build the fire to cook their daily meal, bundles of the fuel tied to their backs or balanced on their heads as they bent and gathered. Their grace and elegance never ceased to amaze me. It was always present within them, no matter how heavy or how bulky the load they carried was. I passed a cow and then another as I approached the town's funeral site and saw and smelt the remnants of yesterday's cremation.

As I sat on the step of the tobacconist's, holding the hot metal tumbler of coffee by its cool rim, I looked up and saw a very strange sight, a sight which I noticed was looking directly right back at me.

Although I had initially been a strange sight to the people of Kalitooly, whose town held nothing of interest to attract the foreign tourist, by now I was known to them and an accepted part of daily life, with my white skin, and fair hair, and long white dress, and flowing white dupatta and black sunglasses.

But to the wandering Sadhu, I was something new and different and unexpected.

He came over to me and stood directly in front of me, staring. I stared back.

He was naked, and his thin wizened body was caked in white ash. His hair, a matted blanket of long grey dreadlocks, came down to his waist, and around his waist he had tied a long strand of red string, the end of which hung down past his genitals. His face was likewise caked in a whitish ash and across his forehead, bold and in thick paint, the three stripes of Shiva's trident were slashed. His dark eyes were set deep into his skull, and they blazed like fire.

He stood before me for a long time, each of us gazing into the eyes of the other, mesmerized by this glimpse into another world within the world, another dimension of being, another space within the space, and the collision of two disparate splinters of the life force manifesting together in time and space.

12th June 2021

The cases of the Delta strain of Covid have tripled here in the last week and now account for more than ninety per-cent of all cases. Consequently, the plan to lift lockdown on the twenty-first of June has been cancelled. Hospital admissions though, and deaths remain low, for the moment.

13th June 2021

The tensions in the ashram between the Brothers and Prakash were growing into a palpable thickness in the air.

Yesudas's handsome face was constantly dark with storm clouds, and he grunted and barked at anyone who spoke to him. Brother Joseph's face, likewise, was clouded over and his brow remained lowered over his eyes all day. The other Brothers, who had been in the ashram since the days of Brother Magnus, were also sullen and moody, their usual bright and happy interactions with the guests replaced by a stony silence as they went about their business. It was oppressive, and I had no idea of what lay behind this change in atmosphere.

I climbed the fence and found the Sadhu, deep in meditation on the veranda of his hut. I sat down on the bench and admired him for a while, until he returned from his voyage deep into the eternal Now and greeted me. As he was brewing our chai, I began telling him about my encounter with the other Sadhu, the man of ashen silence, and he looked up from his task, intrigued.

In Kalitooly? he asked.

Yes, I said, beside the chai stall and tobacco shop.

He looked down again, stirring the now bubbling brew with one hand, and fetching the two metal tumblers with the other.

I want to ask about you Sadhuji, I said. About how you came to be a Sadhu, and about your life before that.

He looked up at me, and chuckled deeply.

You ask too many questions Manee, he laughed, pouring the hot liquid into a tumbler, and then pouring the chai into an extra tumbler, holding it high in the air as the scalding liquid flowed down into the cool tumbler.

He repeated this process four or five times before handing me the now cooled chai, and began doing the same with his own drink. It was an art form which I had not mastered, and my only feeble attempt at cooling tea in this way had been met with a hot sodden mess all over my dress.

I looked at him as we sat sipping on the veranda.

Sadhuji, I said, I really want to know.

Manee, he replied, what I once was is no more, it has passed away like death into the flux of change which is the destiny of all life and all forms; it has dissolved again, back into the formlessness from which it arose, and I cannot speak of it, for even to speak of it is to re-embody it back again into the world of form.

Oh, for heaven's sake, I said. Just tell me.

After our laughter had subsided, the Sadhu looked at me again, and said,

Very well Manee. But first of all, let me explain to you the vision you saw yesterday in Kalitooly, in the form of the naked man of ash.

This man whom you saw was, and is no more, and yet he lives. In this lifetime, it is his destiny to wander the earth naked and ashen and without friend or family, without home or shelter, without clothes or belongings. He is in this world, but he is not of it, and it is his destiny to wander through it like a waif thrown up by the life force, the life force which desires to witness itself through the unencumbered gaze of one who is without desire and who knows no fear, one whose vision has been freed from the grasp of these twin pillars of impulse which are yoked to the five senses, and is crystal in its clarity.

He is thin because he eats only one small meal a day, which must be given to him by a stranger. He is clothed in ash because to become ash is the destiny of the body, and by clothing himself in it now, he has died to the body before the occurrence of his physical death. He is silent, because silence is the highest form of truth. He has no identity because all identity is maya, or illusion, and all forms of identity keep us trapped within the world of change and blinds us to the changeless realm within which all change takes place.

Oh goodness, I said. That *is* extreme.

We both rolled about in laughter, startling a flock of birds in the forest which suddenly flew up as one, wings flapping wildly in the air, and flying off towards town, as we clutched our bellies in pain and wiped the tears from our eyes.

And you, I said, who are you?

I am nobody, he replied.

Mister Nobody, I said. Tell me who you were when you were Mister Somebody, Mister Nobody?

Sadhuji stood up and rearranged his dhoti.

Let us walk Manee, he said, leading the way from the clearing of his hut and into the forest.

In my previous life, he said, I was a Psychologist, a Clinical Psychologist, and a professor at the big university in Madras. I taught students, I wrote books, I saw patients. I was good at it, and because I was good at it, I enjoyed it. I had the approbation of my family and friends, my students and patients, my colleagues, and my readership. My name was Professor Chinmaya Krishnaraj, and Professor Krishnaraj was both loved and revered in his community.

I noticed this change from first to third person in his speech, and felt that he was, once again, distancing himself from the role he had once played.

That sounds like a happy and successful life Sadhuji, I said. Why on earth did you discard it?

Destiny, he said. On the one hand it was destiny, and on the other it was a call, more of a cry, from the deep heart's core to leave it all behind and to live only for God.

And so I did, he continued. I gradually tailed off my clinical commitments and then left my job at the University. I sold my apartment and gave the money to the Sisters of Mercy Mission in Kolkata – these sisters scour the streets, bringing the sick and lame and homeless into their shelter where they nurse them back to health and strength and support them when they move on. Whatever money I had left in my bank account, I gave to my mother, and all my belongings went to my sisters.

Leaving my mother and sisters was the most difficult thing I have ever done, and it broke their hearts. But it had to be so.

I left my home in Madras for the last time ten years ago, taking with me only the clothes on my back, the saffron robes of renunciation, my rubber sandals, a small cloth satchel and a begging bowl. I left behind not only my family and friends, my career and belongings, but also my name, my identity, and all sense of who I had once been.

He stopped walking and turned to look at me. He took my hands in his and looking into my eyes, he spoke sombrely,

Now you know Manee, he said, you must never speak of it again. Chinmaya Krishnaraj is dead.

He turned round and walked back towards his hut, leaving me alone in the forest.

I sat down on the trunk of a fallen tree and gazed into space for a while. As the light through the eucalyptus leaves flickered here and there on the ground and in my eyes, I began to wonder to myself,

Who am I? Am I Marney McDonagh from Drumknock, or am I someone else? Or am I no-one, just like Sadhuji?

My mind was an empty and peaceful blank space as I moved through the forest, shafts of light through the trees piercing the air as I walked, illuminating the path.

Who am I? I thought.

Who am I…?

It was dusk by the time I climbed the fence back into Shanthi, and as I passed by my old hut, I could hear angry voices raised in the distance. As I got closer to the sounds, I began to make out the shapes of some of the Brothers, as well as Prakash, remonstrating with each other and pointing sharp fingers of blame and recrimination.

Old Brother Peter, whose dementia was worsening, stood off to one side, witnessing the trouble and muttering to himself. Now in his eighties, Peter had once been a brilliant student of English Literature, and all that he learned way back in the days of his youth was far more readily available to his well-stocked mind than what he had had for breakfast this morning.

He was forever speaking in verse, and often only responded to others through couplets or quatrains from the greats in the Canon of Literature, or through a snatch of song, or with a wry look and a chuckle at some unseen joke.

As I approached through the darkness, I had the urge to hide myself so that the group would not know that I had seen and heard them behaving in this most unmonastic of ways, and as I was just beside my old hut, I quietly hid behind the shelter of the banyan tree, and watched. Brother Peter stood close to my vantage point, and I could see and hear him clearly in the twilight.

Blow, he was saying, *Blow, winds and crack your cheeks! Rage! Blow! Blow you cataracts and hurricanes, spout till you have drenched our steeples, drowned the cocks!*

Blow and singe my white head thou all shaking thunder, blow and crack nature's moulds that make ungrateful man.

As Yesudas's voice rose above the others, shouting at poor cringing Prakash, Brother Peter raised his walking stick into the air, and shaking it, he muttered,

Aye, aye ... The Ides of March has come. It has come

Caesar, he said, but it is not yet gone....

With that, he limped off past the group and back towards his hut to get ready for prayer.

Shortly afterwards, the group dispersed and I was able to make my way back to my hut, unseen.

My head was spinning as I took a bucket bath, dipping the small, handled jug into the large bucket of water and pouring it over my body, soaping myself quickly, and rinsing carefully to make sure that I didn't run out of water before the suds had been washed away.

What on earth is going on, I wondered, quickly dressing, lathering myself in *Odomos*, and rushing up to the temple to claim my space before the Americans arrived.

What on earth is going on?

As I sat down in the temple, I caught the eye of Alan and nodded to him. Leaving my dupatta and prayer books in my space, I went over and whispered in his ear.

Come for tea, I said, tomorrow, three o'clock, my hut.

Okay, he nodded, as the Brothers were entering the temple to begin the service.

Alan will know what's going on, I thought to myself, just as we all began chanting the evening prayer, and I'll get it out of him tomorrow.

The following morning, I awoke earlier than usual, before dawn, and before the Americans had arrived for their morning session. Rather than rising, I lay on the cot, staring upwards through the mosquito netting to what looked like an enormous spider poised on the netting directly above my face. I blinked a few times, struggling to wipe the sleep from my eyes in the pre-dawn light, and to see clearly.

I had stopped smoking before leaving Drumknock, and had been keeping the nicotine cravings at bay by sucking on nicotine lozenges – large, round, white lozenges, saturated in the addictive stuff. Sometimes I would find that, having climbed onto the cot at night and carefully tucked the mosquito netting in, around, and under the thin mat, I still had a half-sucked lozenge in my mouth, and my disgusting habit had become to simply remove the lozenge and push it out under the tucked in netting, onto the edge of the wooden cot.

As I lay gazing upwards, slowly returning to the world from the realm of dream and darkness, my eyes began to focus. Right above me on the netting, as if suspended in space, was, quite simply, the biggest blackest spider I had ever seen. And, stuck to its underbelly, was a large white lozenge.

I blinked a few times to make sure that I wasn't still dreaming, and then screamed.

The noise startled the spider, which scarpered off the netting in a flash and proceeded to zoom around the hut like a thing jet-propelled, eventually scooting out into the open air through the gap at the bottom of the door.

I lay on in the cot, astonished at what I had just witnessed – the biggest spider in the world, and now addicted to nicotine. I wondered for how long it would zoom around the ashram, high on the drug, before it came to a crashing halt. I felt a mild sensation of guilt, almost like a drug pusher who had just hooked another user. I wondered if it would have withdrawal symptoms, if it would be back for more.

As my wakening mind pondered these questions surrounding the spider, I became aware of a deeper thought, a more persistent one, which had been knocking on the door of my consciousness as I slept. I listened for a moment, and then heard its voice.

Who am I? it whispered.

Who am I?

This thought continued knocking on the door of my consciousness as I went through the usual morning routine, and was still singing in my mind as I arrived for breakfast. Brother Peter was there, and unusually for him, he was sitting with the guests as they chopped the vegetables, smiling and chuckling at nothing in particular. For some reason I felt compelled to sit down beside him, and to speak.

Good morning, Brother Peter, who are you?

Ah hahahaha, he laughed, that's a good one! Surely you mean, how am I?

No, Brother, I replied. I mean, who are you?

He sucked in a long breath and curved his torso backwards, raising his head up and closing his eyes for a moment before replying,

I am soft sift, Manee, *soft sift in an hourglass, at the wall fast, but mined with a motion, a drift, and I crowd and I comb to the fall.*

I thought for a moment, and then said,

Egg timer. You're an egg timer, stuck to the wall.

Thank you, brother, I said, and went in for breakfast.

At ten o'clock at the tea circle I spotted Sister Jeevananda, an elderly nun who lived a short distance from Shanthi, and who often visited. I sat down beside her on the wall.

Good morning, Sister, I said. Who are you?

Jeevananda threw her head back and laughed loudly.

Ah Manee, she said, at last you have arrived in India! But the question you must be asking is not, who am I, but who are you!

Thank you, Sister, I said, and wandered off with the vegetable peelings towards the calf pen, where the hungry rasping tongues of the young cows would be eagerly waiting for their morning treat. As they were wrapping their long pointy tongues around the cabbage leaves I fed them, Brother Joseph came by.

Good morning Manee, he said, stopping to observe me for a moment. With a warm and brilliant smile, he said,

Try to see these calves as they are Manee, not as you are.

Have a bright and blessed day.

Brother Joseph, I called after him as he walked towards the dining hall, Brother Joseph! Who are you? I asked, as he turned round.

Who are you?

He hesitated for a moment before giving out a huge and infectious belly laugh, and then continued on his way.

I stood staring at the calves. How can I not be seeing them as they are, I wondered. They are lovely, soft, baby cows, I thought, and that's exactly what I see.

14th June 2021

When the big hand on the clock sitting on the rickety old blue wooden table reached twelve and the little hand touched three, there was a knock on the door. It was Alan, bright eyed in his saffron robes, bowing down to me, hands together in *namaskar*, and offering me *pranams*.

Oh Alan! I said, bowing back, somewhat ironically, thank you for coming! Sit down, I said, and I'll fetch the tea things.

No need, he said, I've decanted us a flask from the circle. All we need are the tumblers.

I fetched the tumblers from inside and joined Alan on the veranda, where he sat cross-legged on a cushion awaiting his refreshment. I mirrored his position, and sat down facing him, lifting the flask, and pouring us each a tumbler of the thin, sweet brew. This tea was made from tea powder, as it was known, the tea drunk by the tea-pickers on the estates up in the hills and by the poor down on the plains.

Although it was called tea powder, it wasn't tea powder at all. It was dust. The dusty remains left in the bottoms of the tea-pickers' baskets after the tea leaves themselves had been sorted and packaged and sent off to be processed for the markets in India and around the world. While tea lovers in Manhattan and Paris and London savoured the pickings of the poorest daily labourers in India, we in the poorest parts of India supped on a brew made from the detritus of their enjoyment.

Alan smacked his lips after his first sip.

Ah! Good tea! he said.

Well, it's hardly Earl Grey or Darjeeling, I replied, but beggars can't be choosers. It's wet and warm and sweet, and that will have to do us.

Ah, but no, Marney! Alan said. This tea dust of ours has attracted international attention! It's now in demand in all the cosmopolitan cities around the world. And it's expensive there too!

Oh wow, I said. How odd!

What is going on in the ashram Alan? I continued. There is such an air of discord between the Brothers and Prakash. Do you have any idea why?

Alan's eyes widened momentarily. He wasn't shocked by the question, but he was shocked that I had asked it.

I saw them last night, I continued, close to my old hut as I was returning through the forest. They were shouting and arguing. They didn't know that I was there as I had hidden myself, but they were having an almighty row. Brother Peter was looking on, transformed by the scene into Sir John Gielgud's King Lear, shouting his impotent rage at the elements on the blasted heath.

We both chuckled at the thought, and then Alan

said,

Well, there is something of a history between them all you know.

No. I don't know, I said. What is it?

Alan poured himself another tumbler of tea and shifted his position, leaning back against the wall of the hut as he cradled the warm tumbler between both hands. He closed his eyes for some minutes, gathering his thoughts, and then he began to speak.

It took Alan several days and many tumblers of tea to relate to me the long history which lay behind the strained relationships at the ashram. It was a history which stretched back way into Brother Magnus's early days at Shanthi, Alan said, when he was struggling to bring the ashram together into a cohesive whole, setting study programmes for visitors, teaching yoga and meditation, overseeing the dairy and the field work, guiding the novices, and furthering his life's work – to show how it is that the same pure truth lies at the deepest heart of the major world religions, even though this truth has been given to the world through the medium of many different stories which have sprung up at different times and in different places and cultures.

Alan continued talking, taking me back to those distant years in India, when, Alan said, he became aware that despite the fullness of his life, and his inspiring teaching which was opening the hearts of all who heard him, Magnus was deeply lonely.

He had a lot of friends, Alan said, and many of them came to the ashram for long stays, to visit him.

But he was essentially alone, he said, and I could sense a definite pain and longing within him because of this.

I interrupted Alan to remark on how odd it was that Magnus should have had such a love for the writings of D.H. Lawrence, known as the Priest of Sex, when he himself had chosen the life of the celibate.

I recalled how Magnus would often quote passages from Lawrence's novels – The Rainbow and Women in Love – citing Lawrence's descriptions of sexual union, sanctified by the presence of a deep and abiding love, as being one of the ways available to humanity to experience the mystical union with God through this uniting of opposites. I had seen how the writings of Lawrence chimed and harmonized with the contents of his own writings on the dance between opposites, and the eventual unification of opposites which Lawrence wrote of was, for him, a direct route into the experience of the godhead.

I told Alan how I myself had been enthralled by Lawrence's writings whilst studying at university. I had felt that Lawrence sang the song of my own soul, and his belief that deep conjugal union was sacred, echoed what I somehow knew to be true, without ever having experienced it. This fascination with the truth embedded in these novels led me to specialising in Lawrence in the last years at university, and to writing my dissertation on the Religious Philosophy and Symbolism within his work.

In fact, it was the discovery, early on in my reading of Magnus, that we both shared this same knowledge and insight into Lawrence, that drew me into a deeper fascination with Magnus himself, and with his vision, and which eventually drew me to his ashram in South India, albeit several years after Magnus's death.

Alan nodded his head in understanding, and just as he was about to continue with his story, Milly appeared round the corner of the hut, bounding with joy and laughter and sitting herself down beside us in the veranda.

Vannakam! she said, using the traditional Tamil greeting.

I've been looking for you Marney, she said. Exciting news! Our two new American friends, Priscilla and Wendy, just *love* your paintings. They want you to lay your hands on their heads too, and make what you feel into paintings for them. Are you up for it? They're willing to pay two thousand dollars apiece, and there are another two in the group who've asked to come and have a look at what you've created so far!

Oh, goodness, I said. That is amazing! Yes, of course, I'll do it .... But I can't be sitting here in an ashram amongst the poorest of the poor and raking in big bucks at the same time. Let me think about it Milly, about how to handle this. There must be a way to turn this into something really good for everyone.

Alan got up and stretched his legs.

I've got to go ladies, he said. I have an appointment in the village with my Indian family – more tea, and laddus.

I'll catch up with you later Marney, and continue with our storytelling.

Milly and I waved him off and sat on on the veranda, thinking about how to manage this sudden surge in the sale of paintings. It felt exciting, and important, and as the following years would reveal, it was definitely both.

16th June 2021

It was several days later before Alan was able to return to my hut and continue with the story he had started, and in the meantime I had been across the road to visit Neil in the Gayathri Offices, and had also met with the four Americans who were interested in the paintings. As a result of these two meetings, a plan was beginning to formulate itself in my mind, a plan of how to combine the artwork with the needs of the people I was living amongst.

Kumar had taken Neil and I in the Gypsy out to the model organic farm in Muzum for the day, and after I had seen around the place, and learned a bit about the processes being taught to the local subsistence farmers – rudimentary drip irrigation, for example, through the use of half coconut shells with a small hole bored into their base, filled with water and placed beside the roots of plants, shrubs and trees, and organic pesticides made from a mixture of cow urine and bitter herbs, and fertiliser made from combining cow dung, urine and milk, known as *panchagavya*, we sat down for lunch in the long shed with the farm workers.

It was a delicious meal, similar to the foods served

in the ashram, but here, instead of metal plates, our food was dished out onto large banana leaves, and when we had finished, the banana leaves were fed directly to the cows. Recycling at its best.

We moved into the farm office after lunch for coffee perked up with shots of Jamieson's, and to rest. There were lots of questions I still wanted to ask Neil, and this seemed like an ideal opportunity.

We lay out on cots made of rope which had been woven back and forth on the wooden frame by hand, making them into beds far more comfortable than the hard wooden thing I slept on each night. They had a softness and spring to them which my body welcomed after the ashram's unyielding beds, and I struggled a bit not to nod off. But I wanted some answers from Neil, and so I resisted the pull of sleep.

Neil, I said. What brought you to the south of India? I remember when we met before, you told me about the sights you had seen in Delhi, and about the events in Patna which had combined to bring you from Dublin to India, but why did you come south? Why didn't you start your mission up North, where what you witnessed drew you to India?

Oh, that's easy, Neil said. I sat beside Kumar on the flight over from Heathrow to Delhi. We talked for eight hours. Kumar told me that he was returning home after a fund-raising trip in Britain, raising money for the work he wanted to do with the Gayathri Foundation. He had all his plans set out and was raring to go. All he needed was the money.

I had no plans and no idea of how I would go about helping, but I did have the money, and so joining in with

Kumar's plans and helping to realise his vision down in the south seemed like a perfect solution to both our predicaments. And the rest is history.

I see, I said. Well, that certainly was serendipitous for you both.

Seren' what? Neil asked, mocking me. You're a fine one for the big words Marney. I think you've had a wee kiss at the Blarney stone.

Marney of the Blarney Stone, he sang, making up words to the tune of the Rose of Tralee, and causing us both much Jamieson's laced laughter on our cots.

And what about women, I asked, and girls? Why are you so interested in helping them in particular? Why not men, or children in general?

Aha, he said. Therein lies quite the tale Marney. Quite the tale indeed.

He lay flat on his back on the cot, knees bent towards the ceiling and hands clasped behind his head. He gazed upwards, into the far distance, and began talking.

Women have a helluva time of it Marney, not just here in India, but everywhere. Not so bad now in the West with women's lib and all that, but in most countries, women are still second-class citizens, not worth as much as men, subservient to them, dominated by them, often abused by them, dependent on them, under-valued, and here in India, often under-nourished. The best of the food goes to the men and boys, the leftovers to the dogs and the women and the girls.

If a girl makes it to womanhood here, her lot is not an easy one. If she makes it.

If she makes it? I repeated. What do you mean, *if*

she makes it?

I was lying sideways now, head propped up on my hand, looking across at him.

Well, you see Marney, he continued. Girls aren't valued here. They're often not wanted at all. With the dowry system, they're a huge burden on a poor family with barely enough to survive, never mind scrimping and saving to scrape together enough of a dowry to get their daughter married, only to lose her to her husband's family.

It's boys they all want. There's prestige in having a boy and great joy at his birth. When the boy grows and marries, he'll bring his parents a handsome windfall in his bride's dowry, and they'll get his bride too, as a live-in servant, fetching and carrying and cooking for them. So they all want boys.

And that spells trouble for baby girls. Big trouble. So big that they often don't survive for long after birth.

Oh God, I said, what do you mean?

Female infanticide, Marney. Female infanticide.

So what? I said. They kill them? They kill their baby girls?

'fraid so Marney, Neil said. I am afraid so.

Shit, I said.

He turned to look at me, my eyes wide in horror, and looked away again.

Yeah. It is shocking, to us, he said, but here it's

not uncommon. It happens all the time. Used to be they would poison the girls, but when the government began clamping down on the practise, began sending out inspectors to collect the bodies for post-mortem, the poisonings stopped because they could be detected. But quickly a new method was found, one which couldn't be detected. A ball of raw paddy would be chewed up into a ball, stuck down the throat of the girl until she choked to death, and then removed, without a trace. That's what's done in the villages around here.

And that's why all of my work is dedicated to women and girls, helping to lift them up and out of this cycle of either an early death or a miserable devalued life. In our projects, it's the women and girls who become the breadwinners in the family, and their lives are improved dramatically – money for food and clothes and fuel and medicine, and a growing respect from others, even if it's often grudgingly given. Old men's habits die hard. But in a few generations, maybe we will see some real change.

Although Neil hadn't realised it, what he had just said had set off something buried within me, something deep, unacknowledged, unspoken, something which utterly terrified me, and as I felt a sense of panic beginning to grip me from the inside, I sat up and said,

Can you take me back now, Neil, please? I'm suddenly feeling really sick.

Sure, he said, jumping up and going off to find Kumar and the Gypsy.

It seemed to me that each day that I spent time with Neil,

I would learn something new and shocking, something which would blow my mind and leave me reeling for days, and now it had happened again.

Given that late abortions were carried out in their millions every year in the Western world, abortions beyond the date at which the baby could survive outside of the womb, I didn't know why this slaughter of newborn girls should affect in the way that it had. But it had. What Neil had told me felt deeply personal. It had reached right down into my own womb like a metal claw of death, and it was squeezing the life out of it.

But it felt like an old pain, an old anxiety, an old terror, one that had been with me for as long back as I could remember, and which flared up now and then to cripple my mind with fear and fill my body with tension and pain. It had always sent me into a place like despair, but this time, I decided, I was going to fight back. I was going to do something to save these baby girls. If I can save just one of them, I thought, this life of mine will not have been in vain.

Milly had called round with three of the American women, and one Canadian, who wore an annoyingly short fringe. Now into the third and final month of their retreat, they had begun to secretly break out of their silence, having whispered conversations on the steps of the library and behind the meditation hall, and now four of them had come to my hut.

They refused tea, being slightly on edge lest Prakash should wander by and catch them, and they really just wanted to see the paintings, have me lay my hands on their heads for a few moments, and place their orders.

I had told Brother Joseph about the Americans and the paintings, and said that I would like to donate the monies they paid for them directly to the ashram itself, and he had been delighted. The ashram farm was in a need of a new tractor and some new equipment, and the money raised from the paintings would just about cover all the costs, and help bring the ashram farm into the twenty-first century.

Yesudas, who was the Treasurer, was lifted out of his dark and heavy mood by the news, and could now be seen going around Shanthi smiling and laughing with the guests and singing to himself. The Americans had been instructed to pay the money directly to him, and Milly had got the ball rolling by going into the bank in Kalitooly with him that morning, and transferring two thousand dollars into the ashram's account.

Shortly after the Americans had left, Alan appeared around the corner of the hut, springing up the three steps to the veranda in one, and handing me the flask of tea and bowing, before he sank into the lotus position on the cushion and began talking.

Ready for episode two? he said.

Indeed I am, I replied, fetching the tumblers and sitting down opposite him.

Alan continued relating his story, a story which had unfolded during his own first visit to the ashram, as a young man of nineteen years.

I was one of those lucky ones, he told me, who was healed by the outflowing of Magnus's unconditional love, straight from his heart and into mine, and by the Christ-like touch of his presence, which lifted everything and everyone around him into a higher dimension. It was like being in the presence of a living saint. He seemed to be beyond human somehow, and existing on a higher plane of being. He automatically reached out to all those who were in pain – physical, mental, spiritual, and his love was like a medicine.

I once saw him with a young man of around thirty years, he continued, come down south from Bombay after being discharged from a mental hospital up there. The story was that the treatment he had received there had left him in a worse condition than before, and in desperation he had taken to wandering around the ashrams of the Indian South, seeking comfort and relief from what felt to him like the ravaging of his soul by countless demons.

I watched from the side of the temple as Magnus greeted him, he said. The man, Mahesh he was called, was standing alone, swiping at the air and telling his invisible tormentors to clear off and leave him alone. Everyone in the ashram had become afraid of his mad rantings, and no-one went near him. But when Magnus saw him, his eyes filled with tears, and he walked over to the demented Mahesh.

I saw him take both the man's hands in his own, and holding them gently, he began singing a soft and sweet lullaby, gazing deep into Mahesh's troubled eyes. Mahesh was silenced by this, and just stood gazing back at Magnus for a long time, until Magnus embraced him, wrapping his arms around him, and rocking him back and forth like a baby.

They stood like that for some minutes, Alan said, and when Magnus eventually stood back and looked at Mahesh, his face was no longer a rictus of tortured agony. It was soft and calm, and he beamed a magnificent smile at Magnus, before Magnus bowed down to him, and walked on.

That's what Magnus was like, Alan continued. A living saint.

Everyone loved him. Everyone wanted to be close to him. Everyone wanted to spend time in his company. The Brothers themselves would jostle and vie over whose turn it was to take him his tea, or who should be allowed to deliver the many letters which arrived for him each day from all over the world. The only one who was immune to this sense of rivalry was a very young and fresh Brother Joseph, who was happy to simply be in the ashram where Magnus was.

As Alan paused in his story, I poured us both some tea and sighed.

God, I said. I really wish I could have met him. But he had already died before I had even heard of him. But I will say this, Alan, I do feel that he reached out to me from beyond the grave, at a time when I was in a dreadful state of anxiety, depression, even despair. In that state I definitely felt his presence close to me, and seemed to hear his whisper in my ear,

Come to Shanthi Ashram Marney. Come to Shanthi.

Indeed, it was so clear, and the sense of his healing love so powerful, that immediately after that I did indeed begin planning this trip, and, as you can see, here I am!

We both smiled and sat in silence, sipping our tea. A sweet breeze came in over the paddy field, rippling its surface like an ocean, and cooling us as we sat, and I could have sworn that I heard a whisper on that wind, a voice which I knew to be Magnus's, saying

Welcome home, Marney. Welcome home.

Alan got up from his cushion.

Same time tomorrow Marney? he said, and I nodded.

He gathered up the tea flask and his cloth satchel, slipped on his sandals, and disappeared around the back of the hut. I sat on for a while, in a reverie, remembering how it was that Magnus had seemed to come to me after my darkest night, and held out the hand of hope, the hope that there was a good life for me, in India.

The next morning, as Milly and I sat chatting at the tea circle, Yesudas came roaring into the ashram in a brand-new jeep, waving and smiling broadly at everyone as he parked his vehicle at the office, wiping a few specks of dust from the dashboard, and polishing the wing mirror.

Good morning, ladies! he shouted over to us, before disappearing inside.

Milly and I looked at each other.

Are you thinking what I'm thinking Marney? Milly asked.

Slowly, with my mouth hanging open, I nodded my head up and down.

I'm going to follow up on the tractor and farm equipment with Brother Joseph, I said. If he has done what we think he's done, then there will be no more painting money handed over.

But hold on a minute, I continued, thinking.

Maybe, just maybe, a new jeep was at the top of the list of needs, above the tractor ... Let's see, let's not be too quick to judge Milly – after all, we're here to get rid of all those bad habits, and I know that I'm *very* guilty of jumping to conclusions, very often the wrong ones!

Yes, Millie agreed. I'm very guilty of that too!

19th June 2021

Coronavirus is now being worshipped as a deity in some of the Uttar Pradesh villages up in northern India, with villagers doing puja to Coronavirus, and offering it flowers and sweets. I understand their impulse and need to pacify what must seem to them like an angry God.

Here in Britain, almost all cases are now of the Indian variant, and as news of this is broadcast, coverage of what is happening in India herself has stopped.

The lifting of lockdown restrictions here has been pushed back to mid-July, but who knows what will have happened by then, and who knows what variants are cooking themselves up in unvaccinated bodies. Time will tell. I really thought that we'd have a summer of freedom before any new variants would appear in the autumn, but that hasn't happened.

20th June 2021

Back in Shanthi a new group of guests had arrived from England, all of them posh retirees from the Home Counties – Buckinghamshire and Surrey and Berkshire. They were very keen and excited about their trip to Magnus's ashram, and some of them had even met Magnus when he had travelled to England to give talks. They were glowing with enthusiasm for their trip of a lifetime, just before they became too old to make such an arduous journey and withstand the rigours which the Indian climate imposes on the body.

They were well kitted out with sturdy arch support sandals and socks, mosquito repellent, khaki shorts and shirts, hats, and all of them had a head torch strapped to their foreheads for the night-time trips to the temple.

Because this new group had arrived, Brother Joseph decided to teach his course on the correspondence between the *Upanishads* and the teachings of Jesus of Nazareth as recorded in the four Gospels. He had taken up where Magnus had left off in terms of the almost identical truths which seemed to lie at the heart of both the *Upan-*

ishads and the Gospels. I had already heard this teaching, but felt the need to refresh it in my mind and deepen my understanding of it, and so I joined the group for the daily talks.

The meditation hall was kitted out with fifteen new chairs, plastic, with backs and arm rests, and little footstools to accommodate the ageing bodies of the new guests who couldn't manage to sit cross-legged on the floor, or if they could, as some tried, they had great difficulty in getting back up again, and a few of them had toppled over with the effort.

There was a great atmosphere in the hall after all the guests had arrived and settled down, and Brother Joseph had swished in, barefooted and in white kurta and dhoti, the clothes of the ordinary man. He refused to don the saffron robes because, he said, this too represented an identity, even if that identity symbolised the relinquishment of all identity.

After Brother Joseph settled on his cushion and closed his eyes for a few moments, he looked up and invited the group to join him in the *Om Sahana Vavatu* chant, a chant typically made before *Satsang*, or truth seeking, between a teacher and his students.

Om sahana vavatu, he began,

Saha nau bhunaktu

Saha viiryam karavaavahai

Tejasvi navaditamastu

Maa vidvissaavahai

Om Shanthi, Shanthi, Shanthi

The meaning of this prayer is a request to God to protect both teacher and student, to nourish them together and give them energy to make their studies enlightening, and to dispel any animosity between them, bringing peace.

He began his first talk by referring to the *Rishis* of ancient India, those men, and some women who, having completed their roles in society – marriage, having and raising children, working to earn a living – removed themselves from the world to live in the forest, where they were to spend the rest of their lives seeking knowledge and truth about God.

The root of the word *Rishi*, he explained is *rish*, an ancient Sanskrit word meaning, to flow quickly, to glide, to push, to thrust, and with the addition of the suffix *i*, the word comes to mean a person who has attained to Truth and Self Knowledge by those means.

These *Rishis* lived thousands of years ago, and what they learned out in the forests was handed down through the generations by word of mouth, until eventually being written down in what are now known as the *Vedas*, *Veda* being the Sanskrit word which means knowledge and wisdom. This happened around four thousand years before the birth of Christ, and the wisdom which they contain was written down and recorded over a period of one thousand years.

Brother Joseph detailed for us the names and contents of the four *Vedas*, each of which has four parts, the final parts of each one being known as the *Upanishads*.

Although this word literally means "to sit at the feet of an enlightened master", Brother Joseph explained to us that for our purposes they are better understood as the end of the *Vedas*, the end of the search for truth, and represent the Truth to which the *Vedas* point.

The history of the *Rishis*, the *Vedas* and the *Upanishads* is a long and complex one. It is filled with wisdom and truth and is rich in the insights and intuitions which the early *Rishis* gained through their inner spiritual work of purification and contemplation. Brother Joseph did a marvellous job of simplifying it all down to its bare essentials, in order to make the correlations between these and the teachings of Jesus of Nazareth plain and simple.

As he finished the first teaching session, he told us that in tomorrow's session we would look more deeply into the content and meaning of each of the four *Upanishads*, in preparation for examining their corresponding parts in the Gospels.

After the talk, we all filed out into the afternoon sunshine, smiling and nodding at each other, and while some of the English guests chatted in small groups, Yesudas came charging excitedly towards me, from behind Magnus's old hut.

Manee, Manee he said. I want to show you something!

Tonight. After supper. Meet me at the tea circle. Bring Milly.

We will have an adventure!

I was taken aback by this newfound affection and friendship coming from Yesudas, and welcomed it as in keeping with the quicksilver fluidity of his artistic temperament.

Yes, I said, we'll see you then for an adventure, just as long as it doesn't require me to sit on a motorbike!

He threw his head back and laughed loudly.

No, no, no, Manee, we will take the jeep!

When I got back to my hut, Alan was already there, settled down on the cushion with tea flask at the ready. I quickly got the tumblers, poured the tea, and settled down beside him for episode three of the story which was to explain the ashram tensions.

This was my very favourite time of day now, when the heat of the sun had cooled and the sweet breeze from the river over the paddy created the illusion of a vast swaying ocean of green, and a great stillness and quiet seemed to settle over everything.

Back then, Alan continued, the love flowing from Magnus seemed to infuse everyone and everything with a quiet joy. He was such a beautiful man – tall and well-built and dressed in white flowing robes, his long dark hair and beard, curiously unchanged in colour from the days of his youth, his ruggedly handsome, lightly tanned face.

He was inherently humble and this humility of his was plain to see, even in the way he walked, unassumingly, from his hut to the temple and to the dining hall.

He carried in his person an immense silence, and within that silence there was such a fullness of what I can only describe as bliss, and this bliss radiated out from him, blessing everyone and everything around.

Curiously, though, Alan continued, and despite all the joy which his presence brought to others, I could see and feel that Magnus himself was suffering from a deep sense of aloneness.

However, things began to change for Magnus, Alan said, after a young visitor arrived at Shanthi from Varanasi. He wanted to retreat from the world for some time in order to decide on his future path, he told Magnus, and had felt drawn to come to the ashram and live there in solitude until his path became clearer. Magnus accepted him, blessing him with the new name of Sebastian for the duration of his visit, and welcomed him into the ashram. He could stay for as long as he wished, he told him, and wished him well.

I became quite fascinated with Sebastian, Alan confessed, and took to watching him every day, at prayer, in the circle, in the dining hall, and I soon became aware of *his* fascination with Magnus. As I was watching him, Alan laughed, he was watching Magnus! One day at tea I plucked up the courage to ask him about it, and was startled as he blushingly stuttered out his confession that the communion with God which he saw so clearly in Magnus, was what he himself desired.

To see him living and moving, just as he is, in this pure and mystical union with the divine, Sebastian had said, his magnetic blue eyes burning with desire, and to watch his deep communion with all of the nature – the trees and the flowers, the birds, the breezes, the sounds from the forest... I cannot bear it. I cannot bear to see it, to feel it, and not to *be* it.

As the days went by, Alan said, I continued to watch Sebastian watching Magnus. Sometimes he would watch him from a distance, from behind the trees and shrubbery, and sometimes closely, during prayer in the temple, or in the tea circle, or in the dining hall. His dazzling, intense blue eyes never left him.

But Magnus never seemed to notice.

Then one day I saw Sebastian approaching Magnus outside the temple after midday prayer, and overheard as he asked for a private meeting. Magnus, ever bountiful in all his ways, agreed to see the young man alone in his hut at tea-time, later that day.

There was nothing unusual in this, Alan continued. Even I had several private meetings with Magnus, alone in his hut, telling him about what had troubled me, what had led me to Shanthi, and receiving in return his graceful understanding, his guidance, his loving attention.

And actually, Alan said, I really believe that it was during those meetings with Magnus that I was healed from all the mental and emotional anguish that had drawn me here in the first place. His gracious presence, his deep compassion and understanding, the absence of any judgement from him, the love pouring from his deep grey eyes, all combined to wash away the pain of a lifetime. Those times with him renewed me, allowed me to accept myself, to eventually love myself, and move on from the crippling thoughts and ideas and feelings which had bound me.

And as I watched him with Sebastian, Alan said, I understood that something of the same process was happening with him, and I simply gave thanks for the privilege of being here, and for witnessing another healing process as it began to unfold.

It wasn't until some time after this that I began to notice the changes taking place within Magnus, Alan said. As his meetings with Sebastian grew in frequency and duration, he himself started growing even softer and more open, more joyful, less alone. And Sebastian was also changing, his solitude deepening into an inner space where Magnus alone was permitted entry.

It wasn't until years later, Alan continued, that I gained some insight into how Magnus had experienced Sebastian's arrival, and what the deepening friendship between them had meant to him. In the journals which he left behind, he wrote of the blessing which the young man had brought to him in the form of his friendship, and how their deepening bond had begun to heal the loneliness which he hadn't even realised was within him, and led him to experience a true sense of wholeness.

Just then, Babu the *dhobi* arrived with the laundry, all freshly washed and ironed and folded into a neat stack. As I went to get the twenty Rupees to pay him, Alan got to his feet to leave.

I'll go now Marney, he said, and come back tomorrow for the final episode!

I sat on on the veranda for a long time after Alan and Babu had left, gazing out over the paddy vacantly, and allowing Alan's tale of Magnus's young friend to settle. It was a beautiful story, and I could imagine the comfort which Magnus and the young Sebastian found in each other's presence. I felt glad for Magnus, that he had, towards the end of his life, been blessed with this friendship which had healed the deep loneliness which had gnawed at his soul, and which had brought him such a sense of wholeness and completion.

I thought of my own deepening friendship with the Sadhu, our long afternoons together in his hut, his kindness to me and the patience of his teaching. Now that the days were becoming hotter, we had taken to resting inside his hut after our practise.

I would sometimes bring fruits to him from the market in Kalitooly, mangoes and pineapple, and he would cut these into small pieces with great care and offer the pieces to me, placing them into my mouth. And he would bring flowers which he had gathered in the forest, as well as long strands of pungent jasmine from the market, and we would braid the flowers into one another's hair.

His hut was unusual in that it had three long narrow windows, parallel to each other, and reaching from the floor of the hut to the ceiling, all covered in mosquito netting. These windows allowed a cooling breeze to flow into and through the hut, and shafts of light and shadow poured inside and played together on the floor.

On my last afternoon with the Sadhu in his hut, I had massaged his head and curling ringlets with the jasmine scented pomade I had brought from London, from the massage course. I sat cross-legged on the mat, my back resting against the cushion behind me on the wall, with his head resting on my lap, as I worked the pomade into his hair, massaging his scalp and then his face.

He was so beautiful to me, stretched out on the mat, in deep relaxation, and before I knew what I was doing, I bent over his face and rubbed my nose against his. He raised his arms upwards and caught hold of me, pulling me downwards into an embrace which seemed to contain everything and nothing, all at once.

The whole world stopped in those moments. I ceased to exist as a separate being, and so did he. There was nothing in the universe, nothing at all, except for this embrace, between the Sadhu and I, which was a thousand kisses deep.

3rd July 2021

With the success of the vaccination programme here in Britain and Europe, we are now enjoying a summer of sport. The European Football tournament, which had been scheduled for last year, is now taking place, and it seems so odd that now in 2021 we are enjoying Euro 2020. And the tennis is on at Wimbledon, since last Monday, with stellar performances from Djokovic and Federer, the old man of the sport at almost forty years of age, and from our very own Andy Murray.

I love our Andy, not only because of his strength of will and courage in his personal struggles to be the best, but because of the trauma he endured as a young boy in Dunblane. I remember so clearly the day on which it happened – the thirteenth of March 1996. I had been teaching at the time, and had gone to the huge photocopying centre in the college to hand in the following week's handouts to Jim the Technician for copying. His face was ashen when I arrived, and he said,

Have you heard what's happened in Dunblane?

No, I said, what's happened?

A massacre, he replied, in the primary school

there. A madman broke into the school armed with something like a dozen guns – shot guns and rifles and God knows what. And he shot everyone. Or he shot as many of the kids as he could, and some of the teachers. Then he shot himself.

When the story was eventually reported in full, we learned that this man's name was Thomas Hamilton, and that he lived in Dunblane. He had been removed from his position as Scout Leader in the tiny village after complaints of inappropriate behaviour towards some of the young boys in his group had been made. These allegations were that, as well as having taken photographs of the boys in naked and semi-naked states, he had then had two of the boys sleep with him in his van.

His response to this removal from office, was to walk into the school gymnasium and open fire on the children. He shot sixteen of them dead in the gym, as well as their teacher, who, when found, could be seen to have used her body to shield her pupils.

Outside the gymnasium at the time was the next class scheduled for P.E. that morning, and they witnessed what happened. And in that other class was a very young Andy Murray. Like the other witnesses of this horrific and violent massacre, the young Andy was traumatised by it.

As he grew into a man and poured his energies into becoming the best tennis player he could, reaching the top tournaments in the world, and then reaching the semi-finals and eventually the finals, he began performing an odd little ritual at the end of each win. Immediately after the winning shot was played and he was declared the winner, he would look up into the sky and point there, gazing upwards for some minutes, before bowing to the cheering crowds and throwing them his wrist bands.

I always suspected what he was doing, and these suspicions were eventually confirmed when, after winning several Grand Slam tournaments, Andy revealed that he was looking up and remembering his dead schoolmates from all those years ago.

6th July 2021

True to his word outside the meditation hall, Yesudas came for Milly and me after supper, beaming and laughing and full of joy, and ushering us both into the back of the brand new ashram jeep. Pradeep the driver, a handsome, well-built young man from Paripalli, was also beaming and clearly excited to be driving two of the foreign guests off into the dark of the night for an adventure.

It was a clear night and the sky sparkled with a million stars, and the moon, which always seemed bigger and closer in India than in Drumknock, was also beaming down benevolently on our little group. It was exciting, and mysterious, and Milly and I were thrilled to be going off on this jaunt out of Shanthi and into the unknown.

We're going to Kalitooly, Yesudas proudly announced, but not to the Kalitooly which you know! We're going to a different Kalitooly, and you will be amazed!

The drive into town was a hair-raising experience. I had never been driven through the Indian roads at night-time before, and, to my horror, many of the vehicles belting along the roads were without lights. I squawked at Pradeep to slow down, stay on his own side of the road, and caught my breath over and over again as we swished past some unlit vehicle, swerving at the last moment, only just avoiding a head-on collision. Pradeep and Yesudas were thrilled at the screams and squawks from Milly and me, which only served to encourage them to drive even faster and more outrageously.

We eventually arrived in the crowded streets of Kalitooly in one piece and parked the new jeep down a side street, Milly and I already exhausted and awash with relief at having arrived without incident.

Yesudas charged on ahead of us, leading the way.

Follow me! he shouted, and Milly and I dutifully trailed along behind him, pushing our way through the teeming streets and straining to keep him in our view.

We walked for what seemed like an age, all the way through the busy little town and out the other side of it, and onto a wide dusty street, which was even more packed with bodies than the town.

The noise there was an assault on the eardrums, and colourful costumes, and pungent smells, and thronging crowds pushing this way and that, amongst them huge carnival floats, topped with a variety of gods, all bedecked in fine clothes and garlanded with marigolds and roses and jasmine and a multitude of flowers whose names I did not know, and deafening drums, some of them massive kettle drums, and trumpets and bugles.

There were thousands of people thronging along this wide dusty road, and cows and goats and bullocks and oxen, all painted in bright colours on their horns and faces and bodies, and garlanded with flowers, as they milled around in their docile way, mingling with the crowd.

I saw, off to one side of the crowd, what I first thought was an elephant, a very small elephant, with its mahout proudly straddling its shoulders. But upon closer inspection, I found that it wasn't an elephant at all. It was a bull. A grey bull. Its owner had cleverly fashioned a makeshift elephant trunk and a pair of ears from old grey clothes, and had attached them to the poor bull, turning it into a hilarious parody of an elephant.

Yesudas caught our attention and pointed to a huge float on top of which there was a large black and gold god, sporting a big red dot surrounded by a golden circle on his forehead. The float was bobbing about like a ship on rough water, above the sea of swaying heads, and looked in danger of toppling over at any moment.

We will follow this one! Yesudas shouted above the deafening roar, and charged on ahead of us.

As we began to catch up with the float, pushing our way through to Yesudas, I could see that this god seated on his golden throne and surrounded by flowers was being carried by a dozen strapping young men, stripped to the waist, their toned and smoothly rounded muscles tensed and firm under the weight of their god on his plinth, made of thick bamboo poles.

The young men were proud and gleaming as they carried their honourable load, and I marvelled at the beauty of their forms as we followed them, gasping in horror now and then as the whole divine edifice threatened to topple over into the crowd, as one wave after another of bodies came crashing into the gorgeous carriers.

The float, the god and its carriers, as well as its followers, eventually reached its destination – a huge open barn-like structure off to the side of the road. When we came into its view, I peered inside. It was dark in there, and lit by burning torches and many small candles placed before and around a massive centrepiece. There were flowers and flower petals strewn everywhere, and incense burning, and a packed mass of humanity staring silently above the deafening din of the musicians' drums and trumpets, now reaching fever pitch, as the float slowly moved into the barn.

I managed to squeeze inside and found a place directly in front of the centrepiece, shielding my ears with my cupped hands against the din. Before me on a raised platform was a serene black goddess, gazing outwards dispassionately, draped in gold and red taffeta and bejewelled in sparkling gems on her neck and arms and hands, and sitting on a golden throne, with many layers of floral garlands radiating out from the perimeter of her seat. Standing to her right was another deity, a black god, stern and austere as he surveyed the crowd.

The people inside the barn pushed and shoved at one another, creating a path and a space in the centre, and the huge float at last presented its load to the goddess. The excitement in the barn was almost explosive as the float carriers began moving their god up and down, and from side to side, and back and forth, in a curious little dance before the goddess, looking for all the world like a peacock, opening his feathers and jigging around to impress his hen. The carriers too danced, thrusting their hips back and forth, and shaking their genitals up and down suggestively before the goddess, while her disapproving father looked on.

The faces in the crowd were ecstatic, and passionate eyes burned and blazed at the sight of their god dancing for their goddess in the glow of the fire lit darkness, until at last the dance ended, and the god and his carriers pushed their way back out of the barn and into the starlit night.

Yesudas caught hold of my arm and pulled me out of the barn where I was still standing, awestruck by the scene I had just witnessed.

Let's go, he yelled, pushing through the throng towards the edge of the road.

Milly was holding onto my hand and being dragged along behind us. I looked back and caught her gaze, her eyes huge in wonder and her mouth hanging slightly open as she pushed her way through the crowds.

We reached the edge of the throng, pushing our way through to an open space at the side of the road, and found ourselves facing a long line of fire lit stalls, where all kinds of delicious snacks were being cooked up and fried in massive kadai pans, some of them more than four feet in diameter.

The smells were pungent and spicy and overpowering as potato, and onion, and pepper, and egg bhajis sizzled in pans, crisping up to crunchiness before being ladled out into metal baskets. Big potatoes were being thinly sliced and poured into cauldrons of boiling oil, where they quickly cooked, were removed, and then dusted with hot chilli powder and salt, and placed into cones made from old newspapers. And groundnuts and chickpeas, fried and spiced and salted, were formed into mounds on the stalls.

Let's eat! Yesudas shouted, and we all descended onto the nearest stall, handing over our Rupees and filling our hands and mouths with the hot treats.

Did you like? an elated Yesudas said, and Milly and I, still dazed, nodded vigorously.

I will explain it all to you, he said, and then you will understand.

As we crunched and munched our way through the bhajis and groundnuts, Yesudas told us the story of the Kalitooly goddess and the annual festival of *Poosam*.

Kalitooly, he said, is the proud birthplace of our glorious goddess, whose beauty and power draws into her all the gods in all the surrounding villages. They are in love with her, and want her as their bride. Every year they put on all their finery to dance before her and try to win her hand in marriage, and every year her stern father, who constantly stands by her side to protect her, rejects them all as unworthy. Every year he views them and their dance and their music, and every year, after he has seen them all, he shakes his head and says, No. No-one is worthy. Go home and come back next year.

And so the festival of *Poosam* goes on year after year, and the goddess remains single, and the gods are continuously disappointed.

But, he said, it is a happy thing, and not a sad thing, because if our goddess was ever to marry and consummate her wedding with a god, then in that very same instant, the whole world would come crashing to an end.

Oh, goodness, I exclaimed. The marriage of opposites! They cancel each other out, and so nothing is left!

Exactly! Yesudas beamed, leading the way back through the still thronging crowds to our jeep, and onwards home to Shanthi, dazed and amazed and silent against the brilliant midnight sky.

I lay on in the cot, wide awake and staring up at the mosquito netting and the wooden beams of the roof above my head all night long, still buzzing with all the sights and sounds and smells of Kalitooly. I had never before experienced such an amazement of sensory stimulation, and I was dazed.

By and by the symbolism of *Poosam* began to percolate from my body and into my mind, and once again I was wonderstruck at the truth of it, and at the manner in which this truth was so exuberantly expressed every year in this tiny outlying village in South India.

How this entire universe is upheld by the coincidence of opposites, the male and the female, the black and the white, the love and the hate, the light and the dark, the good and the bad, all the way down into the fundamental building block of the material world, the atom, with its exactly equal number of positive protons and negative electrons, these opposite charges cancelling each other out and making the structure itself into a neutral one, within which the dance between opposites creates the world of form.

And even in the Book of Genesis, the name of God himself contains these opposites – *Elohim*, with the *el* being masculine and *oh* being feminine, and how this God breathes out his spirit to create the human race in, male and female made he them, but he himself contains them both in one. It made me think of Thomas Merton's words, that life is really this simple – we are living in a world which is completely transparent, and God is shining through, all the time.

I lay on in the cot in wonderment, until the first stirrings of dawn flowed into the hut, its growing light dispelling the darkness of the night, and the three loud sharp cries from the peacock just outside in the ashram gardens, awakened me from my reverie.

I rose from the cot early that day, still in a kind of dazed trance as I went through the morning routines, and for a change I took my coffee with me to sip as I sat on the edge of the library veranda, to watch Babu the dhobi at work.

He was as thin as a whippet and dressed only in a Madras chequered loin cloth. His dark skin was taut and stretched tight over his frame, so that the webbing of muscle and tendon and vein, and all the knuckles of his spine could be clearly seen as he dipped and squeezed and then thrashed the clothes he worked on against a big flat stone, scrubbing into them as they dripped their soapy water onto the dusty path, and then plunging them again into the white frothing water teaming up from the ashram's artesian well.

It was an ancient sight that I watched, a sight unchanged for thousands of years, and it was mesmerising. Babu worked tirelessly in the cool of the new morning, lost in the rhythm of his work, and I was entranced by the flow of it, the sounds of the gushing water, the slaps of cloth on stone, the vigorous scrubbing, then squeezing, then wringing, then flattening the damp materials upon the washing stone.

I sat like that watching Babu for a long time, until the ashram workers began to arrive from the village and the old, wizened women gathered their brooms and began swishing them along the dusty paths, carefully moulding piles of fallen leaves and flower petals into little bundles, which were then gathered up into cloth sacks, to be later dried and used as kindling for the cooking fires in Paripalli. They worked slowly and in silence, the grace of their once youthful bodies still apparent in their now bent frames, and their slowed movements.

After breakfast I sat alone on the edge of the tea circle, just watching the slow early morning movements of life, and listening to the sounds of the water, the song of the birds, the cries of the peacocks, the swish of the brooms. I was still in a trance when Julie came from the kitchen, carrying a huge kettle of coffee, placing it in the circle before lifting the beater and banging the gong which announced to everyone that it was time for morning break.

Amidst the chatter of the guests, I could see from the corner of my eye that a beautiful young girl was being presented to Brother Joseph, just outside the office. She looked to be around twelve or thirteen years of age, and was dressed resplendently in a full red sari, shot through with threads of gold and embellished around the edges with fine detailed filigree embroidery.

Her thick black hair was tied back tightly into a long plait which flowed down past her waist, and it was decorated with strands of jasmine and colourful clasps, and on her hands and arms, rings and bracelets of gold sparkled in the morning sunshine. Her ears were decorated with golden cuffs and on her right nostril a diamante *mukhuti* shone. She stood there, as shy as a swan, as Brother Joseph admired her, smiling and laughing in appreciation of her beauty. He caught sight of me watching, and beckoned me over to join them.

I was introduced to the young girl, Sathya from Paripalli, as Brother Joseph announced that today was the birth of Sathya as a woman, and that her menses had arrived.

Is she not beautiful Manee, he said, beaming at me, and I gushed,

> Oh yes! Absolutely stunning! Congratulations Sathya.
>
> What a beautiful young woman you have become!

Sathya's proud mother, Parvati, smiled shyly at us, and led Sathya along the path to show her off around the ashram.

Yet again, I was stunned by life in India. I wandered off alone and found a quiet place to sit beside some unoccupied huts. I continued to sit and just stare into space, absorbing the wonder of it all, without thought, without judgement, just drinking it in, becoming heady and drunk with this world, which was so different to everything that I had known before. Through a gap between the huts, I could see into the forest, where a village woman clicked her quick pink tongue and clucked at her small herd of goats as she moved through the trees, stopping and stooping now and then to pick up some twigs and fallen branches for the fire.

My mind wandered back to my own first period in Drumknock. What a sordid affair that had been – blood on my sheets, lots of it, coming from between my legs and staining my probing fingers, and the dread, the dread of telling my mother, and the shame and guilt of it. She had never explained menstruation to me, and so I believed that I wasn't supposed to know about it, but of course I did. Some of the girls at school already had theirs, and whispered excitedly in small groups, discussing it, and the whole business filled me with fear.

Everything to do with sex was dirty in Drumknock, and we children weren't supposed to know anything about it, and any of us who made reference to it got a sharp clout around the ears and sent off to an early bed, without supper. I knew about it, but dare not speak, and so when I told my mother, I put on an act of being shocked by all this blood, opening my guilty red hands for her to see, and pulling up my nightgown.

Your period has come she said, matter of factly, and led me upstairs to the bathroom.

She told me to wash myself 'down there'. as she fished out an old worn contraption from one of the drawers, and fastened it around my waist. It had long dangling bits at the front and at the back, and onto these dangling things she fastened a thick white cotton pad, adjusting the lines until the pad fitted snugly into my private parts. She then told me to pull up my knickers and get dressed.

You're a woman now she said, so keep well away from boys. They're only interested in one thing. You'll bleed for four or five days and then it will stop. It will come every month now for the rest of your life. Well, almost the rest of your life, so don't worry about it. It's natural.

I lay on my bed, hot with embarrassment and humiliation and shame, and cried into the pillow.

With all these thoughts mingling in my mind, and

the still present buzz in my body from Poosam vibrating below my conscious awareness, I wandered back to my hut and lay down on the cot, gazing upwards for a while, until the delicious swirls and clouds of colour which began moving behind my eyes brought my heavy lids down into sleep.

I saw behind my closed eyes the entire universe, its stars and milky ways, its wide-open black space the canvas upon which massive galaxies, glowing in purples and blues and whites of all shades, sparkling with stars in constellations and clouds of stardust, moved through me, leading me deeper and deeper into itself, and eventually I slept.

Milly knocked on the door at around one in the afternoon, wakening me from a deep sleep.

You okay, she asked, we missed you at prayer and lunch.

Oh goodness, I said, what time is it? I fell asleep after coffee...

We spent a little time reliving Poosam and drinking tea, Milly massaging my feet and ankles as we chatted. This had become a habit of ours – sometimes I would massage her head and neck, and she returned the favour by doing my feet, which I loved.

Do you think Yesudas used our money for the jeep? Milly asked.

Well, I said, I really don't know, but when I asked Brother Joseph when the farm equipment would arrive, he just grunted and walked off with an unhappy face. So,

I don't expect we'll be seeing the new tractor any time soon. But maybe a jeep was at the top of their list of needs, we just don't know.

Two more of the American group want to buy paintings Marney, Milly continued, and I don't think we should just hand the money over, without knowing how it's going to be spent.

I agree, I said. It's not for us to jump to conclusions about how ashram donations are used, but I do think we'd both be happier if we were in control of the future sales money.

I took Milly's hand and looked into her eyes.

Milly, I said, I want to do something to help save baby girls from infanticide. I don't know what to do or how to do it, but that's what my heart and mind are yearning for. Will you help me?

Absolutely! Milly shouted. Abso-bloody-lutely!

We lolled around on the veranda together until teatime, thinking and throwing out ideas, and discussing how to realise our newly hatched plan.

The sale of art to help baby girls in India! What an awesome idea Marney, Milly exclaimed. We need to set up a bank account right away, get your paintings to Bella and Patricia in the American group, and pay in their four thousand dollars.

Can you set up an account in Drumknock?

Yes, I said. I'll email Beth today. She'll do it.

Let's call it Art for India, Milly said, that's a good catchy name.

Yes, I agreed, Art for India it is!

10th July 2021

When we had all settled in the meditation hall and the chant had been sung, Brother Joseph continued his discourse.

Yesterday, he said, we learned about the *Rishis* and the roots of the *Vedas*, and we learned that the sections at the end of the *Vedas* are called the *Upanishads*. Today we are going to look at what are known as the *Mahavakyas*, the four great statements which are the cream of the *Vedas*, the cream of the *Upanishads*, and we will see how it is that Jesus of Nazareth himself went through these four stages of consciousness which they describe during his life on earth.

All of the *Mahavakyas* are essentially saying the same thing – that the individual soul and Brahman, or God, are of one and the same essence, and we become aware of this through a deepening awareness of our own experience of our individual consciousness. We find in the *Vedic* Scriptures that there are four levels of consciousness.

There is the waking consciousness, in which we experience ourselves as an individual being, with a physical body and a personal identity, and this is the first level.

Next is the dreaming consciousness, which is also known as the collective consciousness, and this is the realm of ideas from which belief systems spring, and idealised persons emerge, and where the striving towards ideals begin.

The third level of consciousness is the deep sleep consciousness, which is also known as the universal consciousness, and in this level, all the boundaries created in the second level are dissolved. The ideas generated there and the ideals springing from them disappear, and the consciousness becomes one with all, without distinction, without separation.

The fourth and final level of consciousness is the Divine Consciousness, in which the individual experiences his or her essential unity with God.

Much has been written and said about the nature of this consciousness we speak of, and its different forms, but that is for another day, Brother Joseph said. Today we are going to look at how these four levels are described in the Gospels and in the life of Jesus.

We can see that Jesus is firstly described in terms of the first level, the individual waking consciousness. He is born of a woman, and into a family in which he has a name and an individual identity.

We then see that he and his family are part of the collective consciousness, as part of a community, a society, a way of life, and a religion – Judaism.

As Jesus moves into his ministry, he comes to know himself as universal consciousness, and in this stage he proclaims himself to be the Son of God.

And finally, he moves into the fourth level of consciousness, where he can say that, "the Father and I are One", without distinction, without separation, without boundary. At this stage, Jesus Christ desires his followers to know and experience this truth at the core of their being, and he prays to the Father,

I in them and you in me, so that they may be brought to complete unity....

In Christianity, it is the person of Jesus who is the gateway to union with the Father, with God, with the source of creation and the one who sustains life and contains it all. Jesus offers himself as the indwelling spirit to his followers, and through this indwelling spirit, he creates the access point to unity with the Father.

There were gasps and exclamations from the English guests, as they struggled to comprehend what Brother Joseph had just said, to absorb it, to make sense of the profound truth they had just heard, but which was too much for them to grasp in one go.

Brother Joseph said, tomorrow we will look more deeply into the levels of consciousness, and try to understand what consciousness itself is made of.

Outside in the afternoon sunshine, Brother Joseph waited for me to leave the hall.

Manee! He said, how are you? You have been missing in action today!

Oh, I'm sorry, I said, I fell asleep after coffee. Last night was so exciting that I could not sleep a wink!

He chuckled and laughed.

Ah! So now you know *Poosam*! he said. A very great festival, only in Kalitooly, nowhere else in all of India! It is a wonderful thing – each year all of our villages come together as one and celebrate, and all of the villagers enjoy so much!

This morning Brother, I said. Sathya. I am amazed at how a girl reaching her menses is honoured and celebrated here. It is very different to my own experience, and I found it very uplifting, and so hopeful.

Brother Joseph looked downwards briefly, and then looked up again.

Ah Manee, he said, it is indeed a wonderful thing, but it is not as simple as you think. Sathya *is* being celebrated, but she is also being advertised, as a potential bride.

Oh, my goodness, I said, advertised as a bride? But she is only twelve years old!

Yes, Brother Joseph, said. Sathya is still a child, but her body is ready to bear children, and within one month from now she may be married.

Yet another blow to my mind, yet another dashing of hope that somewhere in this ever-darkening world something was right, something was good, something was as it should be. My own experience of menarche all those years ago in Drumknock suddenly didn't seem so bad after all, and I prayed that Sathya would somehow be allowed to enjoy her childhood for a few more years, before she herself became the mother of children.

19th July 2021

Today is *Freedom Day,* according to Boris Johnson – mask wearing and distancing are no longer required, and all shops, restaurants, cafes, bars and nightclubs will re-open. This, despite the numbers of cases, hospitalisations and deaths being on a steep rise, and despite one hundred leading scientists writing a letter, published in *The Lancet*, to Johnson's government, accusing them of a dangerous and unethical experiment which will result in massive numbers of both acute and long-term illness amongst Britons.

They say that Johnson is not only endangering Britons, but the world's population, by giving the virus an enormous laboratory in which to mutate into something which is impervious to vaccines.

There is no news coming out of India, but Annika tells me the situation there continues to be dire.

20th July 2021

When I think back to those early days at Shanthi, I still have no idea what it was which made Bella of the short fringe and myself into something like enemies for a time. I feel that maybe the fault lay with me, and my reaction to her fringe, or bangs, as she called them. Maybe she somehow picked up on my disdain, because one day she came to my veranda where I sat painting and sat down beside me. She wanted to pick up her painting and get the bank details to pay her money into it, and she stayed on afterwards for a chat.

I heard that you're staying here for six months, she said. I didn't know that was allowed.

Oh yes, I said, I got special permission from Brother Joseph for a long stay.

I want to stay for six months too, she said, and I'm going to ask him.

My heart sank. Short fringe was going to be around for my entire stay ... yikes.

What will you do, I asked her.

I'll paint, like you do, and write, like you do, she

replied.

I have a Diploma in Creative Writing you know. And I've studied life drawing, so this is a great opportunity for me to dive into writing and painting.

Shit!

Oh, I said, that's interesting. Well, you're welcome to sit here with me and paint. I have lots of materials you can play around with. She accepted the offer and began working away with some watercolours.

I know you don't like me, she said. Is it because of my bangs?

What? I said, Your bangs? What are your bangs?

She put down her paintbrush, and pointed to her fringe.

My bangs, she repeated.

Oh, I said, your fringe! No, no, no, I lied, I've got nothing against you or your bangs, honestly!

I could feel the colour rising in my cheeks.

But you could maybe let it grow a little bit so that it's not quite so short, I continued.

I like them like that, she said, her face tightening so much that her lips seemed to disappear into it.

Then that's all that matters, I said, and continued painting. As long as you're happy with it, who cares what anyone else thinks.

She shot me a hard, sharp, sideways glance.

Yes, she said. That's right.

Just then Alan appeared around the side of the hut.

Good day to you, ladies, he sang, imitating Bella's Canadian accent, and we both looked up to welcome him.

Are you ready for today's episode Marney, Alan said, plomping himself down on what had become his personal cushion.

Sure, I replied. Bella was just collecting her painting and getting into the swing of some artwork of her own.

You can take the watercolours and brushes away with you Bella, and I'll get them back tomorrow, I said.

Can't I stay? she asked.

Well, no, I replied, Alan and I are having an ongoing private chat about something personal, so it wouldn't be appropriate.

Bella frowned and began to get up, gathering the art materials she had been using together.

Oh yes, she said, everyone wants to talk to Marney, and walked off in a kind of adolescent huff.

Alan and I exchanged a glance, and called after her to say goodbye.

She's an interesting one, Alan said, opening the tea flask and pouring out our drinks. I've seen her walking to temple in an almost altered state of consciousness, like a trance. It's so interesting to observe how the ashram's super-charged spiritual atmosphere affects people, especially those coming here from the West for the first time. And it's even more interesting to see what it brings it up in them, what things buried in the subconscious mind are released here, and then healed. It's a big process for anyone who spends any length of time here.

Yeah, I said, I also find her striking, and I really don't know why. She just told me that she wants to stay for six months, and do exactly what I'm doing, painting and writing. That feels pretty strange to me somehow, as if she's some kind of mirror for me.

Anyway, onwards to the rest of our story Alan, I said. I'm dying to hear what happens next.

Alan picked up his storytelling from where he had left off a few days previously, recounting how he had witnessed that as the love and friendship between Magnus and Sebastian grew and deepened, so both the old man and the young one began to change, becoming altered by the gift of one another.

It was a wonder to see this, Marney, Alan said, to see the change which had come over Magnus, and to feel the place in him which was once occupied by loneliness being filled with love. And Sebastian. A big change had come over him too. He was settling down more comfortably into himself, into his body, into his being. The intensity in his eyes still burned there, but it felt whole now, no longer yearning and searching and desiring, but fulfilled and quietened.

Gosh, I said. How beautiful this is Alan! And how lucky were they, to find each other, to find this incredible friendship?

Well yes, Alan continued, they were lucky, and their friendship did endure to the end, despite what happened next.

What happened next? I asked.

Well, Alan continued, pouring us each another tumbler of tea, what happened next wasn't pretty, but it was very human.

Back in those days I was in the habit of chatting with all of the Brothers during my long stays – their welcoming warmth and friendship was a big part of the healing atmosphere in the ashram, and I loved and appreciated each and every one of them for their loving presence, and their wholehearted embrace of me, and the part they were all playing in my own healing journey, and the healing journeys of so many others.

So when I saw that they were becoming distressed by the growing friendship between Magnus and the newcomer, my heart was breaking for them. They told me in private that it was making them feel overlooked, left out, cut off from the attentions of Magnus, from the bright circle of his love. It was clearly unbearable for them, and I understood their anguish over what must have felt to them like an abandonment, a rejection by the one whom they all loved the most, and they couldn't handle it. But they couldn't leave it alone either. It was an impossible situation, and there was no good solution to it.

I overheard two of the Brothers speaking quietly together outside the back door of the kitchen one day, he said, arranging a meeting in the yoga centre to discuss the situation. And so I crept up there at the appointed time, and hid behind the shrubbery so that I could hear what they were saying.

Oh, you old rogue, Alan, I squealed. That's exactly the kind of thing that I would do!

We both rolled around laughing for a while at Alan's audacity, his nosiness, his determination to listen in on the secret meeting.

I had become somewhat in awe of Alan, seeing him as really quite saintly, an example of someone from the West who had come to India and found themselves, so to speak, and I frequently despaired over how far ahead of me on this journey he was, and wondered if I'd ever catch up. So this admission of his to less than saintly conduct came as a relief. Maybe there was hope for me!

Well, I certainly hope that you're going to tell me what they said, Alan, I said, urging him to get on with it.

Alan chuckled and laughed at how thrilled I was at his boldness, and continued on with the story.

Basically, they gave vent to their pent-up frustrations, he went on, their annoyance at the amount of time Sebastian was spending with Magnus. Magnus was *their* leader, *their* teacher, they said, and now their beloved teacher, the source of their spiritual guidance, had been hijacked by this young upstart.

It was very sad, actually, Alan said, listening in on them, because after all their distressing emotions had been expressed and their anger spent, the real source of their agitation became clear. They all just wanted to *be* Sebastian. They wanted to be in the company of Magnus as Sebastian was, to pray and meditate with him, to speak with him, to share all the little details of their lives with him. When they saw this place for which they all yearned being taken by a rank outsider, they couldn't bear it.

Gosh, I said. I can actually feel their pain. I would have felt the same way – abandoned, rejected, left out, cut off. I don't think I could have borne it either.

Yes, I could understand them, Alan said, understand their distress. It must have felt like an abandonment to them, a rejection by the one they all loved the most, and they couldn't handle it. But they couldn't leave it alone either. It was an impossible situation, and there was no solution to it.

Because they could find no comfort or consolation in the predicament they were in, they began questioning the rectitude this friendship, trying to find something or someone to blame for how they were feeling. At last they agreed that it wasn't a healthy friendship, that there was something disturbing in the connection between the two, and eventually Sebastian became the scapegoat upon which they loaded all their unbearable emotions.

In the following days, still distressed by the painful emotions expressed at the meeting, one of the Brothers broke ranks, and challenged Sebastian about his friendship with Magnus, even positing the notion that he was luring their leader into some kind of sexual liaison. This startled Sebastian, and came as shock. Magnus was equally shocked when he heard what had been said, and with a breaking heart, he agreed with Sebastian's decision to move on from Shanthi and continue his spiritual journey at another ashram

Alan was actually crying as he reached this part of the story, and had to get up from his cushion to walk around the gardens and clear his head.

There's a little more I need to tell you Marney, but

not now, I'm just too sad. I'll see you again tomorrow. I'd like you to know about Magnus's reflections on all that happened between himself and his beloved friend, reflections which continued and endured right up until Magnus's death.

I waved Alan goodbye, and stayed on outside on the veranda, watching the dance of the paddy and the graceful flight of the egrets in the forest beyond, and wept silently until the gong sounded for tea.

23rd July 2021

I was sitting in the tea circle, watching the coconut pickers as I waited for Kumar to collect me in the Gypsy for a trip to Gayathri's orphanage and school in Ramapalli, a village around twenty miles away.

The coconut pickers were a marvel to watch. Thin as matchstick men and dressed in Madras chequered loin-cloths, they scarpered up the coconut palms, as lithe and agile as monkeys, using only a thin band of rope between their ankles for grip, plucking the massive green coconuts, bigger than a rugby ball and a similar shape, and throwing them down to the ground, where they landed with a thud. Then they scarpered back down again, and onto the next palm.

Brother Joseph came by and picked up one of the heavy fruits, beckoning a worker over to chop the top off with his machete, and then handed me the fruit. I didn't know what to do with it, so he asked the worker to chop the top of another, and then he held it high in the air, tilting it forwards, catching the clear liquid flowing from it in his mouth.

Now your turn Manee, he said.

Somewhat anxiously, I held the fruit up in the air, and aiming for my open mouth, I tilted it forward and waited until the delicious juice of the coconut landed in my mouth and on my dress, causing Brother Joseph some hearty laughter.

Just then a distraught young man came running in through the big ashram gates and fell at the feet at Brother Joseph, crying and pleading with him in Tamil. Brother Joseph grunted and led the man into the office, where I could see him opening the small green cashbox and giving the man a five hundred rupee note. The man looked at Brother Joseph, and at the note, and back again, still pleading. Brother Joseph opened the box again, and handed the man another five hundred Rupee note, and was rewarded with a grim smile from the man, who pocketed the money and ran off.

He tells me that his mother has died, Brother Joseph explained, and they do not have the money for her funeral. We give what little help we can to the villagers, but sometimes they abuse this.

After Brother Joseph had returned to the office, Alan came by and stopped for a chat, just as Kumar's vehicle was entering through the gates.

I meant to tell you yesterday Marney, Alan said, I meant to answer your first question, about why there's so much tension in ashram these days. The story I've been telling you, about what happened all those years ago, it must seem unconnected to your question, but it's not.

Oh goodness, I laughed. I'd completely forgotten

about my question!

Well I hadn't Marney, Alan replied, I hadn't. It just took me a while to get there.

We both laughed, and then Alan continued,

That young man, Sebastian, whose presence caused a split in the community all those years ago, that young man is Prakash.

Oh what! I exclaimed, really?!

Yes, Alan said. Sebastian was the name he was given for the duration of his stay, but when he left here, he reverted back to his original name, Prakash.

And so you see Marney, to finally answer your question, it's those old wounds from back in the days of Magnus which are causing the tension. The wounds have been buried, but they've been buried alive, so to speak, and they're still there, still festering, still causing pain and suffering. The Brothers who remain here from Magnus's time have never recovered from their feelings of rejection, and so every five years, when Prakash comes from America, those wounds are re-opened and the old animosities play themselves out all over again, like an ugly festival. Yesudas was the one most wounded by the seeming rejection, and though he has since grown into a fine monk, he's not immune to being seared all over again by the pain of the past, and of acting it out, despite his best efforts.

As I climbed into the Gypsy beside the beaming Kumar, I could hardly get my head around what Alan had just told me. I was amazed that I was living in such close proximity to the man whose love and presence had brought so much joy to Magnus in his old age, and whose absence had broken his heart.

Now more than ever I wanted to hear the end of Alan's story, and learn about Magnus's reflections on his friendship with the young Prakash, reflections which continued for the rest of his life.

26th July 2021

On the drive to the orphanage and school in Ramapalli, Kumar chattered excitedly in his broken English, bursting with the news he wanted to share.

Wait Manee mam, you will see, you will meet, so nice lady, she Neil lady Manee mam, very lovely, very beautiful, very kind. You will like.

Oh, goodness, Kumar, I said, Neil has a lady?

Oh yes, Manee mam. Neil is having one lovely lady! She is Irish lady Manee Mam, she is red of the hair and very lovely, very plumpy. You will see. She is always making the funny Manee Mam, always making the laughing and the joking. You will be liking her, Manee Mam, you will be liking her! She is so very, very plumpy Manee Mam, very much the cuddling lady – when she cuddles so nicely you disappear into her plumpy. It is so nice Manee Mam, so very, very nice.

As Kumar babbled on with his exciting news, and as the Gypsy bumped along the dirt tracks leading to the Gayathri Orphanage and School, my mind wandered back to Alan's visit the previous day. I had seen Prakash after breakfast and had looked at him with a renewed interest, now that I knew his long history with the ashram, and more specifically, with Magnus.

He must have been a beautiful young man. Indeed, he was still beautiful – gentle and muscular, with an inner glow which seemed to light him up from the inside, though now his dark tumbling curls and ringlets were flecked with silver, and some fine laughter lines fringed his big, soft yet intense, blue eyes. I smiled at him as we stood together at the long washing trough outside the dining hall, rinsing our plates, then dipping them into the basin of hot soapy water, giving them a little rub with the cloth, and then plunging them into the basin of clean hot water, before placing them on the drying rack.

Good morning! I said, brightly, hoping to engage him in conversation, but just as he turned around to me, Yesudas came barging in.

Good morning Manee! he said, loudly. Your carriage awaits! Come with me!

As he led me away from Prakash, he stopped and said,

Manee. You must not speak with the Americans. Not at all. Not ever. They are in silence and do not wish to be disturbed. You must respect this and not interfere with their long retreat.

Okay, I replied, flatly. I just wanted to wish him a good day.

No need Manee. Every day is a good day, don't you know? Enjoy your own good day with Neil and the Gayathri people. Go now.

Bloody Yesudas, I muttered to myself, as I gathered my satchel and water canister from my hut. I wish he would sod off. He's the one who's interfering. I continued muttering as I climbed into the Gypsy. I wish he would just sod off and mind his business.

We heard the hubbub coming from the school before we could see it – the shouts and yelps and laughter of fifty children, ranging in age from infancy to fifteen or sixteen years old, all released from the classrooms and into the heat and dust of the central play area to run around for ten minutes before lunch was served.

They played all the games I remembered from my own school days – long skipping ropes, with a child at either end cawing the rope, and a third child skipping up and down in the middle, avoiding touching the rope with her feet, and then running off as another child ran into the centre, and began skipping.

There was a line of five girls all waiting their turn to skip, and when one of them caught her feet in the rope, she had to stop being a skipper and become a cawer, releasing one of the cawers into the skipping line. They sang a lively Tamil skipping song, and each skipper had to jump in the middle for one verse of the song, before running off to re-join the end of the queue.

There were other girls playing at balls against one of the brick walls inside the shelter. They each had two rubber balls, the size of tennis balls, and as they stood about two feet away from the brick wall, they bounced one ball and then the other onto the ground at such an angle that it bounced up against the wall, and bounced back off the wall, and into their waiting hand, before being bounced again.

There were ten stages of bouncing, beginning with a simple bounce off the wall and back into the hand, and going through ever increasing levels of difficulty. In the second stage, the ball had to be bounced from behind one raised leg, then the other, then from behind one leg which was crossed over the other leg, and vice versa, then from behind and through both legs, which were set akimbo, and then on to the grand finale – *big birlie*, where you had to bounce the ball, and then twirl your bodies around three hundred and sixty degrees, returning to your original position in time to catch the returning ball.

If you dropped a ball during any of these stages, then you had to begin the process all over again, from stage one.

Watching the girls play ball brought back my own memories of being a child in Drumknock, playing ball against the wall of the house in the back garden. Oh, how furious I would get when I dropped a ball and had to begin again. Even way back then, as a child, I could be heard cursing in the garden as I picked up a fallen ball and began the game all over again, with grim determination to make it all the way up to *big birlie* without dropping or missing a returning ball.

And other children played hopscotch or peever, or beds as we called them, on a pre-painted tarmac section of the ground, kicking the empty shoe polish tin onto the square marked One, then hopping to the box on one foot and kicking the peever onto the box marked Two, then landing with both feet akimbo, one foot on box Two and the other on Box three, kicking the peever onto the single box number Four, and so on.

The infants and toddlers had been left to their own devices in the sand pit, where they played with colourful plastic buckets and spades, making little sandcastles which promptly collapsed as they brought both their chubby little hands down onto them, patting them back into flatness and playing at running the fine sand through their fingers.

And the older girls stood around in little groups, showing off their stitching to one another – some had made little floral print aprons with bibs and shoulder straps and pretty ties which fastened around their waists, and others had stitched quite exquisite patterns onto thick card. It was embroidery really, but with large stitches, stitched on to pre-printed card. Some of them displayed brightly coloured peacocks, and others red and gold flowers, and others showed a cricket bat and ball. They were all very proud of their handiwork, and chattered excitedly as each in turn showed off their work.

I was still standing beside the Gypsy, watching the girls at play, when a lively red-headed woman came bounding towards me.

Ah be God, Marney! You must be the very Marney

herself! Aw but to be sure it's good to meet ya at long, long last. And what a bonnie birdie y'ar Marney! Sure, tis no wonder the way my Neil has been going on and on about Marney of the pale blue eyes with their luxury of gorgeous curling black fringes! Yer a sight for sore eyes, Marney! Yer a sight for sore eyes!

As she grabbed hold of me, wrapping her thick

arms around me, I felt myself, as Kumar had intimated, disappearing into her plumpy, where I stayed for a long time until being released again back into the day.

Come away in, she said, taking my arm and bustling me into the office facing on to the playground.

You'll be needing a wee refreshment after your journey.

Now, she said, will you be having a wee cup of tea, or would you prefer coffee, or something cooling, as they say hereabouts. Some coconut water maybe, or how about a nice cold buttermilk all spiced up with the red hot chillies! 'Tis a drink will cool you down and heat ye up all the same time. And there's not a body in all of India will make you hot cold buttermilk the way our Vasantha does!

Oh, I said, a hot cold buttermilk, please! That's what I'll be having!

I was feeling quite excited by the presence of this bustling Irish redhead, and try as I might, I couldn't get a word in edgeways as she sat me down beside the whirling floor fan and continued talking, her red curls bouncing along with the animation of her chatter.

I've only been her two weeks Marney, and already I'm suffering with this heat. Now wait a minute, wait a minute, I'll be getting yay yer cooling cup now, and getting a wee one for myself an'all.

Off she bustled, leaving me alone in the office, and a quick glance around the room told me that there was a lot of filing to do, and a lot of paperwork undone, and waiting in high piles on the desk.

There! she said, bustling back into the room and

plonking herself down on the chair beside me.

Now Marney, she said, Neil tells me you're here in India looking to be transformed. Is that right? You're wanting to be, now what was it that he said then, aye, you're wanting to be cleansed, and then purified, and then transformed. Is that right enough? That sounds like one o' them cycles on me auld washin' machine back home.

I laughed out loud.

But is that true enough, Marney, she continued, what Neil says, that you're wanting to be transformed?

Still laughing, I nodded my head.

And what are you wanting to be transformed intae? Sure, you're lookin' like fine swan to me already. Are you wanting to turn back into a duck?

I opened my mouth and just laughed and laughed at the banter of this fine Irishwoman, who was such a tonic and an unexpected blast of irreverent effervescence from the Emerald Isle.

Oh, goodness, I said, it's wonderful to meet you, whoever you are!

Whoever I am? she said. Do you not know who I am? Has that old rogue Neil never mentioned me name to you? That'll be just like the man, all wrapped in himself, and all wrapped up in his lovely Marney! I'm his sister for God's sake, I'm his sister, his big sister, and I'll be giving him a clip around the ears for his insolence, the cheeky wee monkey, never even mentioning me name.

I'm Nora, Marney, she said, Nora Shaughnessy, though me old man Seamus Shaughnessy, who gied me his name, passed away some years ago, leaving me with an aching heart, a pocket full of money, a big house, and a lot of time on me hands. So here I am now, helping ma wee brother Neil o' the tatters do his good work amongst some of the finest souls God ever crafted with his holy hands. Thanks be. Thanks be.

Oh, I see, I said! By the way Kumar was talking, I thought you must be Neil's wife.

Neil's wife! Nora said. That's a good one! Neil's wife! No, no, no, Neil's never had a wife, not even a long-term girlfriend, and that's why, when we all heard him talking about Marney, Marney of the pale blue eyes, our hearts were fair singing and dancing and leaping about for joy, for Neil, God bless him, despite all his flaws and failings, and God knows he has them aplenty, has never had a serious wumman in all his life.

Oh, I see, I said. That's so funny! How good it is to meet you Nora, you're a tonic, and a real blast from home!

Aw, now thank you Marney, Nora said. And God alone knows, but I'm very glad to meet you too. Fancy that Neil, never even mentioning me name. I'll be having words with him.

You've a lovely name, Nora. It's one of my favourite Irish names, I said.

Oh Nora, Nora said. Well, there's a tale behind the naming of the wumman you see seated beside you Marney. 'Twas me old man, Kieran Kavanagh, a Dublin man through and through, and by God did he idolise our very own Bard, the James Joyce himself. He read every word that the Bard ever wrote, and then he read them all again, and then he read them all again, and again and again and again. Sure, whenever he was speaking to us babbies, we never knew, 'twas it Kieran Kavanagh whose voice we heard, or 'twas it the voice of the James Joyce who lived within him.

He idolised the James Joyce so much that when God saw fit to bestow him with the grand gift of a bouncing baby girl, there was not a moment's hesitation between me own good self appearing on this god forsaken planet and me old man running off the registry office to pronounce himself the proud father of the brand-new Nora, named after the good wife of the James Joyce himself.

And then he was aff to the pub, buying drinks for all and sundry, singing and dancing and reciting all the stories he knew about his idol from all his days in Dublin.

Oh, goodness, I said, what a character your father sounds like! And I never knew that James Joyce's wife was called Nora!

That she was Marney, Nora said. Nora Barnacle was her name, and me old man always used to say that, with a name like that, she was bound to stick to him.

We both roared with laughter as Vasantha, a pretty young girl in a golden sari and the longest black plait, glided into the office, carrying a metal platter on which two glasses of spicy buttermilk sat sweating their condensation onto the tray.

I quickly downed the spicy hot cold drink, thrilling at the delicious sensations of cold, cold buttermilk and hot, hot chilli peppers, smacking my lips, and calling after Vasantha for another one. Vasantha turned around, flashing me the most gorgeous of shy smiles, delighted that her drink was so appreciated, and bowed her head quickly before disappearing through the doorway to fetch me another one.

Is Neil not around, I asked, as Nora downed her drink and wiped the white moustache of foam around her lips with the back of her hand.

No, she said. He's away up in the north for a few days. There's some work that needs doing up there, and he says he's the man for the job. He's never been work shy in all his natural has our Neil, but I'm thinking that what he has on his mind is a wee bit too dangerous, even for the heartiest of Irishmen. There are dark days up in the north, and even darker dens of iniquity, and our intrepid Neil has his heart set on entering into this godforsaken darkness, and saving some of the poor souls in torture up there.

But I've warned him aff it Marney, it's too dangerous, even for a man o' Neil's wit and courage. Far too dangerous.

What kind of work is it Nora, I asked, suddenly serious again, and why is it so dangerous?

Just then Vasantha returned to the office with two more large glasses of her incredible drink, and announced that lunch was being served in the canteen.

Please come now, Madams, Vasantha said. All the girls are so thrilling to see you! They cannot be containing themselves with the excitement!

We quickly drank down the buttermilk and followed Vasantha along the dust path and into the canteen, where we were greeted by fifty beautiful girls, all lined up in their best clothes, smiling and laughing and breaking out into a high-pitched Tamil song of welcome.

3rd August 2021

The Sadhu had been very interested to hear all about my visit to the orphanage and school.

It is very good work these Irish people are doing Manee, he said. Very, very good.

And what about you Manee? Do you have some plan for your life after your long ashram stay is complete? I know you must return to your native place in July, for your visa will expire, is it not? What is in your fine mind Manee? Have you listened carefully, in the deep silence of your heart, to hear the words of God, to know what is required of you according to His will?

Well, Sadhuji, I replied. Now that I have completed almost five months of this long stay, I must confess that I've begun wondering what I'll do after my time here is completed. I know that Neil and Gayathri would like me to join them, helping to run the orphanage and school. They know of my qualifications and experience in education, and they feel that I am the perfect fit to join them there. But for some reason, my heart isn't in it. I've been so happy at Shanthi. I have learned so much. And I have met you, and this is a very great gift to me.

Sadhuji smiled contentedly, satisfied by this admission.

And I've also managed to gain some space between the me who was suffering so badly in Drumknock, who really didn't want to live any longer, and the me who is emerging here in India.

Let us speak of your former self Manee, Sadhuji said, for she is with us still, and still she suffers. You are simply distracted from whatever troubles her by all the newness you have found here in India. But she is still here, and she still needs our attention.

Something deep down in my gut began churning as I listened to the Sadhu, and I felt the familiar visceral twist, like a metal claw of torture, gripping and squeezing my bowel, and I struggled to breathe for a moment.

You see Manee, the Sadhu said, I can see her, and I can feel her, and I know that when I call on her, she is immediately present here with us. You have simply buried her for the moment, but she is not dead. She lives. She is in pain. There is something deep down, unspoken, unacknowledged, unknown to your conscious mind, which continuously tortures her. It is your most urgent mission Manee, here in India, to begin to try to rescue her from whatever it is which is torturing her soul. I am here with you, Manee. I will help you.

Oh God. The churning deep within me began in earnest, and I could feel the tendrils of the anxiety which it sent up from its core, spreading throughout my intestines, shortening my breath, and a sensation like panic began to take hold of me. These were all sensations which I had become familiar with throughout life, but during this time in India, with so much to distract me, they had become quiescent. But here they were again, back in force.

Oh God Sadhuji, I said, you're right. There is something buried in me, something which terrifies me. It flares up every now and then, and it can really debilitate me. Many times in the past it has led me into deep depressions, panic attacks, suicidal thoughts. And I really don't know what it is, where it comes from, what it's all about.

I know my dear Manee, the Sadhu said, I know. I can feel it, and sometimes I can see it, in your eyes, whenever you are startled, whether it be the sudden cry of the peacock, or the flight of the birds, or some unexpected sound which interrupts our discourse.

Yes, I replied. I have always been very easily startled, even by the slightest thing, for as far back as I can remember. Even as a child.

I see Manee, he said, I see, and I hear. We have between us now the beginning of insight. We know, for example, that whatever is ailing you from within is a very deep wounding, so very deep that it goes all the way back down the path of your lifetime, and into the infant whom you once were, and who you still are, for you see Manee, the child within us is the deepest part of ourselves, and the most truthful and authentic aspect.

It has been said that the child is the father of the man, he continued, and also of the woman, and this is more truthful than we realise, for the child is the very foundation stone of our personality, and when the child suffers a wound which does not or cannot heal, then the adult cannot be formed according to its true nature. The adult will be formed around the wound, and much of its energy will be spent in guarding and protecting this wounding against further wounding, and also against being discovered by others in the outside world.

As I sat crossed legged on the mat facing the Sadhu, listening to his words, the panic within me was rising to a fever pitch, and everything within me wanted to get up from the mat and run out the door and through the forest and never stop running.

I know Manee, he said, that my words are causing you some disturbance, and that you would now like to run away. But you must not. These feelings which are being stirred within you, we must allow them. We must not become afraid of them, we must not fight against them, we must not run away from them. We must find our courage Manee, and we must face them.

Let us sit in silence for a few minutes and simply allow these feelings to be, without judging them, without doing battle with them, without trying to avoid them. Just allow them to be.

I closed my eyes, focussing my attention on my breath, the in-breath and its sensations in the nostrils, and the out-breath, and its sensations in the nostrils, and allowed all the distressing emotions which had taken hold of my viscera and all my organs, and even my muscles, which had begun shaking, to simply be.

As my breath became deeper and more even, I was able to sit with the feelings and even able to feel the feeling of wanting to run away, without panicking, and eventually I opened my eyes again.

Very good, Manee, the Sadhu said, very good. You have learned something of the art of meditation and this art will become your most important tool as we begin to explore whatever it is which is buried within your unconscious mind and that has been causing poor Manee so much pain.

The Sadhu took me in his arms and hugged me so close that the breath was squeezed out of me. He held me like that for a long time, before releasing me.

Come again tomorrow Manee, he said. Together we have much work to do.

I staggered back to my hut, catching my dress on the fence as I climbed over it, creating a large tear along the hemline which tripped me up as I trod on it, landing me face-first down on the thorny path, scratching my hands and face and skinning my knees. I clambered clumsily back up onto my feet, noticing the metallic taste of blood in my mouth from my cut lip, and walked quickly on along the path, managing to reach the hut and get inside and bolt the door without being seen.

I sat on the cot hunched over, arms wrapped around my torso, and cried. I didn't know what had just happened with the Sadhu, but I did know that I was back, yet again, in that place which I had so dreaded throughout life, a place of horror in which every fibre of my being seemed to be screaming out to be rescued from *it*, though I did not know what *it* was. It was a place in which I was utterly cut off from love, and where my soul seemed to be ripped and torn and shredded into pieces by wild ravening beasts.

When I had entered this place previously, I had reached out to find comfort and oblivion in good red wine and this had, at first, seemed to offer comfort, but latterly, back in Drumknock, it had begun to make these attacks even worse, even more ferocious.

I lay down on the cot, entrammelled by this bomb blast from within. Everything that had been me seemed to have shattered into a million disparate pieces which crashed around inside my head, and I knew from past experience that it would take some time for them to come back together, that it would be some days before I could begin to function again, and to be with people.

I must see Brother Joseph, I thought, and tell him that I will be fasting and in silence for three days, so that he doesn't come looking for me. But I didn't want to see him. I didn't want to see anyone. I'll write him a note, I thought, and push it under the office door. It's resting time now, so no-one will be around. I hastily penned the note and, having made sure that the coast was clear, made my way quickly down through gardens, and pushed the note under the door.

There, I thought. That's that done.

I felt a wave of relief wash over me as I turned from the office door to head back quickly to the safety of my hut, when I heard a familiar voice calling out my name. I turned round towards the back door of the kitchen and saw Bella, waving.

Damn it!

I waved back and hurried on.

Marney, Bella called out, Marney, I'd like to speak with you! I've been into town and have bought so much art material you wouldn't believe it! Come and have a look! I've started on a big painting, and I'd like your opinion.

I'm so sorry Bella, I called out without stopping, I really can't talk now. I'll see you later.

As I hurried off, I could feel Bella's eyes burning holes into my back, but I just couldn't speak with anyone. I had to get back to my place of safety, and sit still until this attack began to abate.

At last, I lay down on the cot, rearranging the hard pillow beneath my head for comfort, and closed my eyes. I had been watching my breath for some time, waiting for these feelings of panic to begin to subside, and they had.

As I lay there, my mind returned to the practise which Brother Joseph had taught me, and I began going through the steps of awareness of breathing, of sounds far and near, of bodily sensations, and then the active imagination aspect of seeing the thoughts passing through my mind like clouds passing across a vast, clear blue sky, and rising above the clouds and resting there, facing the sun.

I lay a long time facing the sun. I was tired. I could feel the waves of tiredness washing over my body, washing through my mind, but still I stayed there, above the clouds, facing the sun. The sun was huge and so brilliant as I faced it from behind my closed eyes, and the sky such a vast, vast crystal-clear expanse of blue. And still I lay there, facing the sun.

Suddenly, a tongue of fire flew out from the sun, straight towards me, startling me so much that I opened my eyes.

I closed them again, and lay facing the huge, brilliant sun, upon the vast, vast blue sky. And again, it happened. This time, three tongues of fire came flying out of the sun, straight towards me, startling me again, and I opened my eyes.

Again, I closed my eyes, and lay there, facing the sun, until suddenly, the whole huge, brilliant sun came hurtling straight towards me, giving me such a big fright that I sat bolt upright on the cot.

What the hell! I thought.

I got up from the cot, and went out onto the veranda to sit for a while, to recover from the meditation practise, my mind busily trying to figure out what that had been about. I wondered if it was a good thing or a bad thing, and was just beginning to think that it must be a good thing, some kind of stage of progress announcing itself, when Brother Joseph came around the side of the hut.

Ah, Manee, he said. I have read your note Manee. So, you wish to be in silence for some time, is it? And you wish to be fasting, is it?

Yes Brother, I said, I feel the need, just for a short time, for three days.

Very good Manee, he said, his head wobbling involuntarily as he spoke. I shall ensure that you are not disturbed. Julie will bring you one small meal per day, at midday, and sufficient water.

Thank you, Brother, I said.

As he was turning to leave, I suddenly called after him.

Brother Joseph, I said, I have just been meditating, the practise which you taught me, and have had the strangest experience.

He listened attentively as I recounted the activities of the sun behind my closed eyelids, and was completely unsurprised by it.

Ignore it, Manee, and continue with the practise. These mental activities are intended to distract you from the practise. They are thrown up by some psychic energies which fear that they will soon lose their home within your subconscious mind as you deepen in meditation. Give them no attention. Just continue with the practise. Eventually, they will be burned away and they will bother you no more.

You can think of them like the new movies in America, where you put on three-dimensional spectacles as you watch the screen, and it appears to your mind that the creatures on the screen are leaving the screen and coming straight towards you. You can watch and see how the people scream and shout as they are tricked by the spectacles and by their minds. But there is no danger. It is an illusion. But the mind believes in the illusion, and because the mind believes in it, the whole body and the whole being is fooled.

Do not be fooled, Manee. You are in no danger.

8th August 2021

The three days of fasting and silence passed without incident, and little by little, the symptoms of anxiety and panic began to abate, and all the shattered pieces of my personality, and perhaps even deeper than my personality, perhaps even my ego itself, had reconstellated enough that I was able to be with people again, albeit in small doses, and only with Alan and the Sadhu.

Alan had come by at tea-time on the third day, by which time I was able to speak again, and be in company. And it was good to see his familiar face and be in his calming presence. I knew that he too had had his troubles, and it had been his own troubles which had brought him to Shanthi and to Magnus all those years ago. I also knew that it was his time with Magnus which had brought him to a place of peace and acceptance, and I prayed to God that I too would find at Shanthi the resolution and peace which Alan had. But at the moment that felt like a very distant prospect. The thought of returning to the Sadhu and embarking on the work he had mentioned was terrifying, and I knew that I was not ready for this. I would have to tell him.

It was at around three o'clock on the third day that

Alan visited, allowing me a gentle re-emergence into the world of others following the deep retreat into silence, and I embraced him when he arrived. There was such warmth in his response, and I felt truly held, truly safe in the arms of this gentle, gentleman.

I'm glad to see you Alan, I said.

And you, Marney, he replied, still holding my hands.

I know that something has happened within you, he continued. It's inevitable, you know, that when we come to an ashram like Shanthi for a long stay, there is a reason for it, even though we may not be consciously aware of that reason. There is something in us, deep down, which leads us to where we need to go on this journey called Life, and it's always good to heed it. I think of it as intuition – when you listen to it, when you heed it, when you follow it, it grows stronger, but when you ignore its promptings, it begins to die.

You and I Marney, Alan said, we have listened to it, and it has brought us here. What troubled me was brought to the light of day by the time I had with Magnus, but it didn't reveal itself all at once. It took years for the whole tangled web to loosen, and years more before I could see it clearly. But you are in the right place. A process has now begun, and it will continue until completion, however long that might take.

Alan's words comforted me more than he knew. I knew that I couldn't move quickly into what ailed me without being destroyed by it, and I was very much comforted and consoled to know that I had time, that I could take it slowly, that I could recover from this recent attack and find a place of stability, security, peace, contentedness, before beginning the work which the Sadhu had mentioned. But I knew that I had to proceed with caution and care, and protect myself against any further violent attacks.

I hugged Alan again, and for a long time we just stood on the veranda, holding each other in silence, wrapped and held by a warm blanket of understanding, compassion, love.

Oh well! I eventually said, time to get back to business!

Alan poured our tea from his flask, and handing me a tumbler, sat down on his cushion. We sipped together for a while in silence, gazing out over the paddy to the last puffs of smoke coming up from this morning's cremation.

That's old Thomas, Alan said. He passed away in the night.

Thomas had been our gateman, an ancient fellow crippled with pain and almost blind. We all saw him daily, silently sitting on a battered wooden stool just inside the ashram gates, dressed in the same rags and tatters each day, and wearing a large pair of oversized sandals, coming apart at the seams. They were far too big for his feet, and as he shuffled along to and from the ashram, the sandals never quite left the dusty path. He wore thick spectacles held together by tape, and one of the lenses had been smashed many years before, so that Thomas had looked out on the world in his latter years through a cracked and shattered webbing of glass. I quietly prayed for Thomas, and wished him peace on his onward journey.

A strange shiver ran through my body, as I watched the last wisps of Thomas drifting up from the spent pyre and into the clear space above it, disappearing into the air, and the feeling of the transience of this life passed through me.

It's a tale told by an idiot, I thought, *full of sound and fury, and signifying nothing*. But within that empty nothing, there is everything.

It was a strange day altogether, with me stilled into silence after the passing of the storm and tempest which had raged within, and Alan, so willing and able to meet me there, his heart full of compassion, his mind full of understanding, his presence a balm to my soul.

Some time passed before he took up the story of Magnus again, and I could tell that, as he recounted those days which he had witnessed, he still felt Magnus's pain, and he somehow still suffered along with him.

After Sebastian had left, Alan said, Magnus was bereft, and even his physical appearance had changed. The spring had gone from his step and he was now quite bent, his face more solemn. He spent more time alone in his hut, reflecting in silence and writing in his journal. It's because of these journals which he wrote, and which have been preserved, that we know of his reflections on all that happened between him and his young friend.

Magnus was no coward Marney, Alan said. He was completely honest, completely dedicated to finding the truth in all things, and if there had been any homosexual feelings within the friendship, he would have acknowledged it. He was unafraid to speak the truth as he saw it, for to him there was nothing more important than the truth. Indeed, it's because of his commitment to finding and exploring deep truths that we have his teaching.

Instead, Magnus came to understand that what had happened between them was a love so deep and so warm that it pierced through to their very cores, bursting their hearts open to the love of God, and this is what lay at the foundation of their friendship.

That's so interesting, I said, interrupting Alan, that Magnus and Sebastian, by coming together, created this opening within themselves, this opening which led directly to such a huge experience of God's love.

Yes, Alan said. It is very interesting, and it led Magnus into further explorations of the nature of love, and the ways in which it is experienced by us humans.

He was later to write in his journal on the topic of love, and its differing forms and expressions.

Oh, I see, I said. That sounds fascinating. I'd like to hear about it. They say that love is a many splendored thing, but people never really stop to enquire, in any meaningful way, about all its differing aspects and forms, though I believe the ancient Greeks did, dividing it into two main manifestations – *eros* and *agape*, or the mutual love and sexual union between couples, and simple love of mankind, of one's neighbour.

Yes, Alan said, they did, and it was with that same ancient Greek philosophy that Magnus's reflections began, leading him eventually into an understanding of Platonic love, that divine, soul-connected and asexual love, which can break open the heart. The Greeks called it 'philia'.

Can we talk about that tomorrow, Alan, I said. For some reason, there's something which keeps popping into my mind as I listen to you, and I'd like to share it now.

Sure, Alan said. Share away.

I took a deep breath and closed my eyes for a moment to remember.

It goes back to my first days here at Shanthi, I continued. I knew early on that I wasn't cut out to rise before dawn for prayer – I'm a semi-nocturnal creature, often still awake at three or four in the morning, either painting or writing, and while everyone else is busy with their morning rituals and breakfast and vegetable chopping, I'm still in a deep sleep.

Brother Joseph knew about this, and was happy for me to continue along, in keeping with my own natural rhythms. But I began to feel a bit guilty about never doing the chopping work, and so I asked him if there was some other form of work I could do.

He thought for a while, and then replied that I could tend to the library, sorting out the books and cleaning the dust from them. I jumped at this, and immediately agreed, but then something happened, something which I'm only beginning to understand now. It goes back to about two years before coming to Shanthi, when I was on a retreat with my sister Beth.

I had wanted to support the family whose house the retreat was being held in, and so I went into their tiny gift shop, intending to buy something, but there was nothing there that I liked. I looked around at all the theology books, prayer books and cards, beads and candles, little crosses, and then a small book, tucked away in a corner, caught my eye. I picked it up to have a look. Its title was, *I am With You*, and when I read the blurb, I learned that it had been compiled by an Anglican priest, John Woolley, and it contained messages which he had received throughout his life, during periods of severe depression.

When the messages had started coming to him at first, he would just listen to them, and then later he began jotting them down on whatever piece of paper he could find – a bus ticket, the back of a Cornflakes packet, and so on. As the years went by, he accumulated quite literally hundreds of these short messages, and he eventually decided to compile them into a book which would hopefully help others.

The little book which I held in my hands was this compilation. And so I bought it, without realising at the time how much I would come to rely on the messages, during the times when I myself went through periods of depression. In fact, in the year before coming here, I prayed with the help of this little book both morning and night, but when I was preparing to come to Shanthi, I decided that I would leave it behind. I felt that I had become too dependent on it, and wanted to be open to what India would offer me.

But when I went into the library here on that day, to begin my shift of work, the first thing I saw when I opened the door was this very book, sitting alone on the big desk. To be honest Alan, my heart sank. I kind of felt that it was following me, against my will, and I was annoyed.

I stood in the doorway for a quite a while, just staring at the book, which seemed to be daring me to pick it up and open it, and though I was determined not to give in, I did in fact pick it up, and open it.

The words which I read made me angry. They made me angry because I had been feeling freer here in Shanthi than I'd ever felt, and because during my first few weeks at the ashram, I had become aware of a growing distance between me and all the distress which had led me here. I was truly hopeful, was almost believing that the suffering was now over, but the words which I read made it clear that it most definitely was not.

Golly gosh! Alan said. How curious! How very curious! Are you going to tell me what it said?

I raised my eyes to heaven and frowned.

Yes, I said, I'm going to tell you.

Then go ahead, he said.

I opened the book at random, which is the way it's intended to be used. When you're looking for guidance, you hold the situation in your mind, and whist doing this, you open the book to read the guidance.

So. When I saw the book, and then reacted to it, and then wanted to ignore it, I knew I had a problem. I knew that there was something in it which I didn't want to hear, something so important that the bloody book had followed me all the way to India, and had presented itself to me at the very moment when my work was to begin.

Anyway, I continued, I held in my mind the thought, What's this all about? And opened the book.

The passage began with some words of comfort and consolation before getting to the point, and the point itself came through the words of the book straight into my heart, like a dagger.

It said,

You have to be emptied. This will not be easy, but it has to be done.

I slammed the book shut, replaced it on the table, and left the library. I've never been back there since.

Alan let out a huge laugh, and continued roaring, until he saw my face.

Oh Marney, Marney, he said, consoling me. Don't look so crestfallen! What you read is wonderful! And it's true. You do have to be emptied, become empty, in order that you can be filled, by God! That's why you're here! That's why we're all here!

Still disconsolate, I grunted, yes, I suppose so. But why does everything have to be so difficult?

It wasn't really a question, but Alan chose to answer it anyway.

It reminds me of an old tale I once read, he said, about a man who suffered continuously, and when he asked God why he suffered so much, he was told that in order to be made perfect, all that was impure within him had to be burned away in the fires of love, but that while he could only feel the burning and the suffering, what was really happening was that he was being made into a vessel fitting enough to hold the Spirit of God.

I let out a deep sigh, and threw Alan a look of acceptance, of surrender. For what else could I do?

13 August 2021

The panic attack which I had experienced after the last session with the Sadhu coincided with the realisation that my time at Shanthi was drawing to a close, and the two things didn't seem unrelated. I spent long periods in my hut or on the veranda, painting and reflecting on my time at the ashram.

What a gift India had been to me, continued to be. She had, for many months, given me the time and space to be free from all that I had run to her from, and I felt nothing but deep gratitude for this lengthy respite. I had four weeks left of the six month' stay, and had no idea what I would do next.

Opportunities had presented themselves with the Gayathri Foundation, with Neil and Nora, and though I loved them and the work they were doing, it didn't feel right for me. I still wanted, still needed, the spiritual comfort and direction I had found at Shanthi, and I wasn't yet ready to leave, although I knew that I must, even if it was just for a brief time, in order to go home, renew my visa, and then return.

I also knew that what ailed me continued to ail me, and I was as much in the dark about its roots as I ever had been, and that knowledge filled me with a kind of dread. But the thought of our plan, the one between Milly and myself, to start selling paintings, raising funds to help rescue baby girls from infanticide, was the single thought which kept my head above water. It gave me a purpose, a direction, and a mission, and these filled me with great hope for the road ahead. I felt that if we could work on this, bring it to fruition, then my life would have some meaning. If I could rescue just one baby girl, I thought, then my life would not have been in vain.

It was the thought of establishing *Art for India* back in Drumknock which lifted me up out of the dread of leaving Shanthi. That thought, and the knowledge that I was not done with India, nor she with me, but that our dance together was only just beginning, was the driving force within my last weeks in the ashram.

Bella had come by a few times during those days of reflection. She had been painting in her hut, and was keen to show me her work. Although she continued to irritate me in an irrational way, I was glad to see her beginning to sink down into a deeper place within herself as she painted. One day she came and sat with me, and we worked together in silence for some time, before she began speaking. She wanted to tell me something, but found it difficult to do so.

She had built a hard shell around herself, and a lively active personality was part of that, but the quiet which the painting had facilitated seemed to be allowing her access to a deeper part of herself, and something within that depth wanted to be expressed. I knew that she had a story, and that she wanted to tell it to me.

She told me about her life in Ottawa. It was a life

of wealth and privilege – her father had inherited a large fortune from his father, and had invested it wisely, so that Bella had never wanted for anything. She had attended the best schools, had the best tutors, had her own stable of horses, a fact which startled me somewhat, and even had the beginnings of her own art collection.

She had studied at the University of Ottawa for four years, gaining her Diploma, and afterwards she had become interested in Indian philosophy and religion, studying Sanskrit and practising the chanting each day. She said that the vibrations from the sounds, the chants, were really helpful to her, and it was because of this that she had joined Prakash's group here in Shanthi, to continue her learning and deepen her practise.

She wanted to tell me about her birthday celebration, for her eighteenth birthday, when her father had thrown her a magnificent party. She talked about how the champagne had flowed, and how everyone had supped and danced beside the lake on their property, and how her father had led them all to the front of the house to present her with his surprise gift – a red Porsche Carrera 911, wrapped up in cellophane and banded round with red and white ribbons.

But she never drove that car, she told me, because of what had happened later that night. She told her father to return it to the dealer without telling him why. She had never told anyone, she said, until now.

It took some time for Bella to be able to say what was on her mind, but when she eventually did, it came as a huge shock to me. She had been assaulted at her party, by one of the older boys, but until now she had managed to fool herself into believing that it had all been consensual, and that nothing wrong had really happened. She told me that it had never affected her, although she still remembered it all clearly, but that it had put her off boys, men, and that she had decided never to marry.

She wouldn't allow me to hold her, brushing me off and saying that she was fine, that she had just wanted to tell me about this thing which had happened to her ten years ago, on her eighteenth birthday. And then she left.

This had been such a bolt from the blue, and it took me some time to digest it. It explained so much about Bella, her brittle personality, her odd behaviour, and I realised then that she too was like me, that she had come to Shanthi to escape from something, but that she had brought that something here with her. As had I.

How broken and battered we all are, I thought, as I cleared the paints and brushes away, and left the work outside to dry in the sun. How broken and battered we are.

16th August 2021

I had visited the Sadhu on the first day after my retreat had ended. He had not been surprised that I had felt it necessary to withdraw from the world for a time, and to recover. He listened to me attentively, as I explained to him that I knew that I was not yet ready to undertake the work he had spoken of.

Yes Manee, he said. I know. Whatever it is within you, which is so deeply buried, is not yet ready to show itself. There is a process, designed by nature, to protect us from everything and anything with which the mind cannot cope, which it cannot process. This process, created by nature for our benefit, for our protection, is known as the Defence Mechanisms.

I told you before that the adult which a wounded child becomes is formed around the wound, and the biggest part of that formation is the creation of a battalion of mechanisms which hide the wound from the mind, from the world, and protect it from further wounding.

You have these mechanisms Manee, in abundance, and so far they have served their purpose of protecting you from that which you cannot look upon.

We can see them in your lively humour, he smiled and chuckled, and the way in which you make people laugh, so often and so easily. This humour is a great thing for you Manee, because the big belly laughter allows your being to express much of its energy, in a healthy way. It releases much tension which you hold in the body, and it releases many nice chemicals within your brain, the happy chemicals we call them, and so this wonderful laughter washes you, refreshes you, renews you.

Your art, your painting, and your writing Manee, these wonderful gifts, these you have also been using as tools. Your writing allows you to express what is within you, without interruption, without challenge or contradiction, without others seeing what is in your mind. And your painting, from the unconscious, this allows your mind to simply rest, and become absorbed in the movements of the brush on the canvas, the colours in the paints, the textures which you create, and the interest in the forms which emerge beneath the movements of your hand – all of these things engage your mind in a most healthy way.

And so you see Manee, you have been given incredible gifts, which are also the most healthy of defence mechanisms. You have used them well, and creatively, not only for yourself, but also for the benefit of others.

But Manee, there are other defence mechanisms which are not so healthy, although they do still protect you. I know that you avoid relationships with men, although I can also see that you would like to be married and to have children, is it not?

I nodded. Yes, I whispered.

And so, this dreadful conflict between desire and

avoidance, or aversion, this is most painful for you, for when you move towards your heart's desire, immediately your body and mind, your being, is feeling under threat from that very thing which you desire, and so you must turn away from it. Is it not so?

Yes, I said. It is so.

Very good Manee. Very good. You are making progress. You are now becoming more consciously aware of something of the dynamics at work within your personality, and this knowledge, which will grow over time, is empowering for you, for you see Manee, something which has been hidden from your view, is now coming into your sight. This is the beginning of a very important stage of insight, as we call it, and this insight will help to make you more free.

Thank you, Sadhuji, I said.

I know that what you say is true. I feel it in my bones.

Sadhuji laughed loudly, throwing his head back, so that all his golden curls moved and swayed around like an ocean, and his laughter was so deep and so hearty, that I had no option but to join in. And like the man said, after our had laughter subsided, I felt washed, refreshed, renewed.

Ah Sadhuji, I said. What a tonic you are for me, what a rare and wonderful gift! I never knew, when I prepared to come to India, never guessed when I arrived at Shanthi, what a wonderful treasure I was to find, buried out here, in the midst of the forest!

We both laughed again, heartily and loud, and

then became quiet.

May I speak with you, Sadhuji, regarding my thoughts about the future?

Oh course, my dear Manee, of course! In fact, I insist upon it!

Again, we peeled with laughter, me conscious of the washing, the refreshing, the renewing qualities of this great gift of laughter.

Well, I continued. You know that Neil has invited me to join him at Gayathri, at the orphanage and school. It's such a wonderful project you know. When you enter into it, and see the children, hear their happy shouts and see their energetic games, you know that these orphans are the lucky ones – they are loved and cared for, and all their needs are met. It is a very joyful place, and I must confess that I have been tempted to join them. But as I told you before, for some reason, my heart is not in it.

I see, the Sadhu, said.

What is it Manee, that your heart is in?

Well, I said, you know that female infanticide is happening.

Yes, he nodded, seriously. Yes, Manee, I know it.

Well, I continued. That is what my heart is in. It's in doing something, however little, to help to save some of them from such an early death.

And how will you do this Manee, this noble work? For it is not easy, and you will require many resources.

Yes, I said, I know. But I have the beginnings of a plan.

I see, he said. And what is this plan, Manee?

Well. You know that I've been painting in the ashram, and that some of the American guests have already bought and paid for some paintings.

Yes, he said.

Well, I've set up a bank account back in Drumknock, and the painting monies have already been paid into it. When I go home, I will arrange more fund raising, by having an art exhibition, with not only my work, but the work of fellow artists, and we will gather even more money together.

This is a very good idea, Manee. It will both keep you engaged in your artwork, with your community in your native place, and it will be a start in building up the resources which you will need.

Yes, I said, that's what I also feel. I know that I must always be painting, for that is my greatest medicine, but if I could combine this with some good works for the benefit of these girls, then it would feel like heaven on earth.

Again, we both laughed loudly and long.

Manee, the Sadhu said. I have an idea of how you might go about beginning this project of yours, here in India. There is a woman, an English woman, who lives up in the mountains. When you return after visiting your native place, we will speak of this matter again.

But now, Manee-ji, I think it is time for chai.

19th August 2021

I had been sitting at the tea circle, waiting for Kumar to arrive to take me to Gayathri, and I noticed that one of the older villagers, a thin wizened woman in a tattered old sari, was lying face down in the dust just outside the circle. Whenever anyone came by, she began crying and wailing loudly, attracting their attention and calling after them in Tamil and then, after they had passed, she became quiet again.

Concerned, I went into the office to find Brother Joseph. I knocked on the door and could hear him calling from within,

Come!

I poked my head around the door, and saw him sitting at the desk, typing on the computer.

Ah, Manee, he said. How may I help you?

There's a woman Brother, I said, lying face down in the dust beside the tea circle.

Ah, he said. Yes, yes, yes, I know.

Is she ok? I asked.

Yes, yes, yes, she is okay Manee. She is okay.

Then why is she lying there like that?

Eventually Brother Joseph stopped typing, took off his spectacles, and looked at me.

Ah Manee. Always so concerned for the welfare of others. This woman whom you see lying in the dust. She is the mother of the young fellow whom you saw asking for money, for his mother's funeral.

What? I said.

Yes, Manee. She is that young fellow's mother, and, as you can see, she is not dead, she is very much alive. So much alive is she, that she has come here today to tell me that her husband has now died, and that she does not have the money for his funeral.

Oh God, I said, that's unbelievable!

Many unbelievable things, Manee, are believable here in India. So you must not concern yourself with our poor sister, lying in the dust. She will simply lie there until she becomes hungry, and then she will go home for her dinner.

I returned to the circle and sat down again. Some of the American guests, whose course had now finished, were gathered there with their luggage, waiting for the taxi to arrive to take them to the airport. Their faces were crystal clear and bright with joy, their eyes sparkling after their long retreat, and they were so relieved at finally being out of silence, that they chatted and laughed loudly, exchanging email ids and addresses, and promising to keep in touch.

Three of them, two of the younger men, still dressed in their kurtas and dhotis, and an older woman, with blonde curling hair and a silver-trimmed turquoise sari, grouped together just outside the circle to have their photograph taken. As the American woman, whose name was Amelia, was adjusting the stick-on red bindi between her eyebrows, the village woman lying on the ground looked up, and caught sight of the camera. Immediately her eyes lit, and she jumped up for joy and joined the group, determined to be included in the photograph.

I could hardly believe my eyes at how immediately she had been transformed by the arrival of the camera. The Americans too, who had been concerned about her earlier, were flabbergasted by her sudden change in mood, and welcomed her with open arms and laughter, delighted to have her in their photo.

After a battery of photographs had been clicked, the village woman insisted on seeing the snaps on the camera screen and was delighted by them, smiling and chuckling away to herself and muttering some words in Tamil, before skipping off out of the ashram gates, and back to her home in Paripalli.

As I climbed up into the Gypsy I could see that Kumar's usually bright demeanour was sullied over with a pall of worry.

What's up, Kumar, I asked.

Oh Manee mam, he said. It is Neil Sir. Not yet returning from the North. Nora Mam is most perturbed and pacing, Manee Mam. All the time she is speaking, but she is speaking to someone who is not there, and I am most unhappy, Manee Mam. I do not know what it is that is happening. All the day long I am worry, worry, worrying, what will happen? Will we all go away? How will I feed my family if Neil Sir goes, and Nora mam is no more here?

Och, don't worry Kumar, I said, I'm sure it's nothing serious. Neil Sir will be back soon, and all will be well. They've no intention of leaving Gayathri. Gayathri is their life now Kumar, every bit as much as it yours.

I am hoping that you are correct, Manee Mam. I am *rumba* hoping, Manee Mam. *Rumba* hoping.

When we arrived at the orphanage, all was quiet. The babies and toddlers were at play in the sandpit, now covered over by a huge umbrella to shield them from the fierce heat of the sun. They were absorbed in their sandcastles, building them up and then destroying them with their chubby little fists which came down on them, pat, pat, pat, until they were flattened. And the infants and small children were inside the classrooms, taking their lessons, the faint sounds of them reciting their times tables mingling with the distant sounds of traffic, and the clear song of the birds from the flowering hedgerows.

Kumar parked the Gypsy and led me along the path round behind the low row of offices to the kitchen area, where some of the older girls, under Nora's supervision, were busily preparing lunch in the covered porch of the kitchen proper.

Today's lunch was to be daal, spicy vegetables, chapati and Pongal rice, four of the most delicious dishes.

These girls, some of them as young as twelve and thirteen years of age, were already expert cooks, and I watched for a while as they stirred the daal and vegetables as they bubbled in their cauldrons above the wood fires, tending to the fires as well as to their pots.

Some were kneading the mixture for the chapatis, grabbing a fistful of the dough, wrapping it in flour, then tossing it from one hand to another, then flattening it onto the worktop, before lifting it up again and kneading it into a ball, and throwing this back and forth again, from one hand to the other, before flattening it once more, and finally popping it onto the piping hot griddle, where it shrank and puffed up nicely, before being flipped and cooked on the other side. Already a neat little pile of chapatis was sitting ready for the lunch table.

Nora saw me and shouted out,

Ach Marney, a very good day to you, my lovely girl!

Wait a wee minute, and I'll be right over.

I noticed that Nora had taken to the habit of the village women, and was wearing an emerald green nightie with large orange and yellow flowers on, a little frill of cloth around the buttoned bib and on the sleeves. It was full length, down to the ground, and just beneath its hem, I could see that she was wearing a pair of sturdy open-toed sandals which she must have brought with her from Dublin.

Her face was red with the cooking and the heat, and small beads of perspiration had gathered on her brow and above her lips.

She rubbed her floury hands on her apron, gave them a quick rinse under the outdoor water pump, and came rushing over for a big hug.

Ach, but it's good to see you Marney! How are keeping? And how on God's good earth are ye surviving this infernal heat? I think I'm going melt Marney! One of these days you'll come looking for me in that office and all you'll find is a big puddle, for as surely as God is good, I'm going to melt!

Come away into the office Marney, and we'll sit ourselves down beside that most inadequate of all man's creations, the floor fan. Did ye ever, in all yer life, see such a pathetic wee instrument Marney? Sure, all it does is whizz around, moving the blistering hot air from one part of your body to another. But it's better than nothing I suppose. There's no creature on the face of this earth 'twas meant to survive in this kind o' heat Marney, but here we are, and not dead yet!

We had barely sat down beside the big floor fan, which whirred noisily as it strained against the hot air, when Vasantha appeared in the doorway, carrying her tray of delicious buttermilk, and flashing us her shy smile as she placed the sweating glasses down on the table beside us.

We each grabbed hold of our glass, wrapping our hot hands around its chilling sides, before downing the buttermilk in one go.

Kumar was telling me that Neil isn't back yet, I said, wiping the foam from mouth. Are you expecting him soon?

Ach, Marney. There's a great big tale to be told about our intrepid Neil.

You know, Nora went on, our auld ma and da, when were only wee babbies, drummed the good Lord's teaching into us so thoroughly that it persists within us to this day, and it directs all our actions. If ever we come across another suffering human being, we know it as our bounden duty to reach out and lend a helping hand, for didn't he tell that it is our duty and our purpose here on this earth to love our neighbours every bit as much as we love our own selves, and didn't he also tell us, with his wonderful tale of the Good Samaritan, that it's not just some folks who are our neighbours, it's all folk?

Yes, he did Nora. I was raised in the same way by my own parents. We're here to love God, they told us, and to love and serve our neighbours.

Aye Marney, the Dublin catechism and the Drumknock one will be being the same then, Nora said.

Yes, I said. That's right.

Aye, well, so we'll both be singing from the same hymn sheet, Marney, and you'll have some understanding of what Neil is getting himself mixed up in way up in the North, God help us.

You'll maybe have heard about the darkness up there Marney, and the dreadful traps being set by some of these agents of darkness, to ensnare some of the poorest wee lassies from some of the poorest wee villages?

No, I said. I don't know what you mean Nora.

Ach well, then you must brace yourself Marney, for it is an ugly tale.

For the next half hour, Nora filled me in on what she described as "the dark dens of iniquity up in Delhi". They were brothels, hidden away in the back streets, she said, where young girls and even children, were rented out for sex in exchange for money. These children had been kidnapped from the streets where they had been found wandering and begging, many of them having run away from their villages, in the hopes of finding a better life in the city. Instead, what they had found was hell on earth, as they were drugged and beaten and raped on a daily basis, until they no longer knew who they were, or where they had come from.

Oh God, I said. Oh God.

Aye, said Nora. Oh God, indeed.

So, our Neil. He's up there now, trying to see if he can help these poor lassies. But it's dangerous, for the evil of these agents of darkness, and their love of the filthy lucre, knows no bounds. 'Twould be nuthin' to them, nuthin' at all, to disappear an auld Irish fella who happened to be pokin' his wee sharp nose into other folks' business, and they would snuff him out as soon as look at him, and not give it a second thought. And if the Police came round alooking, sure they'd just bung them a lakh to look the other way.

But we must give our thanks to the Lord Marney, for as luck or chance or whatever you want to call it would have it, Neil, God love him, has met the acquaintance of a wee group of fine young Americans, already working away hard up there, not just releasing the girls, but rehoming them in the lovely blue mountains of the south, not too far from here, and tending to their wounds with all manner of loving therapies, and good food, and exercise in the fresh mountain air, and a wee school just for them.

And they also have some lawyers working with

them, lawyers schooled and skilled not only in American law, but in Indian law an'all, and they're bent on prosecuting as many of these devils as they can gather enough evidence on.

They're up to all kinds of dodges Marney, hidden cameras in the brothels, and all kinds of other James Bond tactics, and according to our Neil, they've quite a bit of solid evidence on three of the dens so far, but they're keeping it under wraps until they have enough for another five Prosecutions.

They don't want to give the game away too soon, if you know what I mean, for if the other scoundrels get wind of what they're up to, then they'll shut up shop and move elsewhere, and the poor wee lassies will be lost forever.

That sounds really wonderful Nora, I said. What great people. And how is Neil helping? What's his role on the whole thing?

Well, as far as we've come, he's no role. No role at all. Not yet. But his busy wee mind is whirring away and coming up with some ideas of his own. For the one thing, he's asked me to be on the lookout for any lands hereabouts which might be available for the buying, and methinks he's hatching the plan to build a wee centre for the girls close by. Now wouldn't that be a fine, fine thing, Marney?

Oh God yes, I said. A very fine thing indeed.

Anyway Marney, that's the tale been told, and you're now as wise as I am in the matter. Our Neil is telling me that he has no plans to return here any time soon, and he's not been shy about asking me to hold the fort until he gets back, and me, with me lumbago, and me bad knees, and the heat, oh my God the infernal heat. I can hardly hold meself up, never mind the whole bloody fort, God give me strength. God give me strength.

It was after dusk by the time Kumar dropped me back at Shanthi, and the place was curiously quiet. All of the American guests had left, apart from Milly and Bella, who had been given permission to stay on to paint and write.

I was sad not to have been able to meet Prakash and chat with him, or even to look into his face, his eyes, so that I might catch of glimpse of the soul whom Magnus had so loved, and whose presence in the ashram had taken Magnus through the gateway of human love, into an ever-deepening experience of God's love.

What a marvellous tale Alan had told me, and what a tragic one. But out of that tragedy, an even deeper level of love had been born, and for that reason I could not feel too sad about it all.

26th August 2021

I sat alone in the circle one hot evening as my time at Shanthi was drawing to a close. I could see Brother Yesudas and Brother Peter off in the distance, stamping along the path to the temple, their footfall loud against the quiet night air, and sending eerie echoes up into the inky black starlit sky. It had become so blisteringly hot now that the snakes had taken to coming out in the evenings to seek the cooling balm of the ashram's irrigation channels, with its little pools of cool water dotting the gardens here and there, and we had all been told to make loud stamping sounds with our feet as we walked along, so that the snakes would hear them and clear off.

Some of the snakes were poisonous, highly poisonous – someone had even seen a Russel's viper – and if we were to surprise one of them, then a single bite from its deadly fangs would see us in hospital, or worse.

It was so odd to sit in the temple, now almost empty of foreign guests, after such a long time of it being so full with the Americans, and the English, the French and Germans and even Argentinians and Australians. Now it was only Milly and me, and Bella, alongside the Brothers. And Milly too was leaving in the morning. I would miss her. Oh god. How I would miss her.

28th August 2021

Alan came round on the eve of his departure from Shanthi, to finish his story about how his encounter with Sebastian had changed Magnus, and forced him to re-evaluate his understanding of love, both human and divine, and to explore the relationship between them.

It was within the ancient Greek philosophy of love that Magnus had found the structure to explore his own new understanding, and Alan explained how Magnus had detailed this new understanding in his journal.

Until Sebastian, Magnus had believed that brotherly love, shown equally towards all, was the highest form of human love, and that it was the celibate life which best allowed this form of love to grow and deepen, eventually piercing the innermost heart, where the pure love of God resided. But after the friendship he had experienced with Sebastian, he came to understand that a mutual bond of loving friendship between two people could have within it an even greater capacity than *agape* does to open us fully to God's love.

By the time he reached the end of his life, his writings show not only this new understanding of Platonic love, but reveal that his thoughts and feelings had come into almost complete alignment with those of the English writer whom he had so admired. Like Lawrence – he at last believed that *agape* without *eros* could not satisfy the fullness of our human nature because it ignored the fact that each individual person is created with a gender which is only one half of a whole, and each half is designed to be always seeking its completion in its opposite gender. To cut off or deny that aspect of our humanity, and ignore our basic nature, he came to feel, was almost an assault on it, and at the end of his life he believed that the best and most wholesome pathway to God was to be found within a loving marriage between a man and a woman.

His journal entries incorporated long quotes from the works of Lawrence, especially those in which he spoke of the transcendence of sexual union within loving marriage, and Magnus concluded that this was indeed the right royal pathway to the mystical experience of oneness with God.

That's so interesting Alan, I said. And it brings to mind that first name of God in the book of Genesis, or the book about how everything was generated by God.

In that name, *Elohim*, we have both the masculine and the feminine mentioned separately, within the structure of the word itself, but because they are both contained within the one word, the one name, they are not separated within it, or within the godhead itself. They exist there in perfect balance and harmony, a perfect whole. It's not until God begins his creation that the male and female are separated out from Him, and in that breathing forth of his spirit into his creation of the male and the female, the whole dance of life and all created things begins, and continues, upheld by this incredible tension between opposing forces.

It's even there within the atom Alan, I said, with its electrons and protons, the two opposite forces which are the fundamental building blocks of the entire universe.

Yes, Alan said, thoughtfully. Yes indeed.

And, I went on, what Magnus came to know and understand after his period of reflection also sheds light on what the Brothers experienced as rejection, because if it's true that human nature is always reaching out to bond in love with one other, and I think it is, then the lifestyle which celibacy imposed on them must have been hard. If it's our nature, our programming, to seek out the other and bond with them in an exclusive relationship, then the manmade rule of celibacy cannot destroy it. It must remain.

That impulse within them, it must have attached itself to Magnus, who became the object of their love and devotion, and when Sebastian came along, so obviously usurping their place in that relationship, then the pain must have been unbearable, it must have felt to them that they were being literally torn apart.

Yes, Alan said. I think that's exactly what happened. It's a salutary tale, with lessons to be learned all around. Magnus learned this deep lesson through his connection with Sebastian, and it changed him. As you say, he came to understand human and divine love in almost exactly the same way as Lawrence did, but sadly, for most others,

I think those lessons have been missed, for the moment anyway.

Well, I said, at least the seeds of the solution can be seen within the problem itself, and maybe one day they will be planted, and grow, and change things in a way that seems impossible now.

Let's hope so, Alan said. Let us hope so. But one thing's for sure Marney. We've both learned that what expressed itself in the Brothers as jealousy and anger, was really their anguish and pain. And it feels good to acknowledge that.

Yes, I said. It does.

As Alan and I embraced on the veranda for the last time, and said our tearful goodbyes, I told him how blessed I had been by his presence at Shanthi, how enriched my life had become because of his friendship, and how my knowledge and understanding of Magnus and his life and his work had been deepened by our conversations, and we promised each other that we would remain in touch, and that we would meet again.

Drumknock is not so far from the Cotswolds Marney, Alan said, nor the Cotswolds from Drumknock, so we have no excuse not to meet up again when you are back home, and I hope that you will visit.

A kind of hollow emptiness began to fill me as I waved goodbye to Alan, and for the first time, the reality of my own imminent departure began to hit home. I had only a few more weeks at Shanthi before I too would take the taxi to the airport, and board the flight which would take me back to Drumknock, and I didn't know how I felt about that.

I felt so grateful to India for all that she had given me, for all the magical, and sad, and exciting, and tragic aspects of her being which she had shown me, and for the love that I had found in her, and for the promise of a deeper and more fulfilling road ahead than I had ever dared to dream was possible. I knew that I would be back again, and that somehow India would bestow upon me the medicine which I needed for the healing of my soul, and that within her embrace I would find wholeness.

29th August 2021

My last days at Shanthi were quiet and still. I saw Bella each day as I walked past her hut where she painted on the veranda. I had deepened and grown in understanding over my months in the ashram, and now felt a natural flow of warmth and love for this young woman. We would smile and wave at each other, and I felt happy to see that she was becoming peaceful, as her paintings developed into wonderful scenes of village life, bright and colourful, full of movement and the bubbling joy which seemed to overflow from the villagers, despite the harshness of the conditions of their life.

She had even allowed her fringe to grow to just above her eyebrows, and the effect of this was quite amazing – it softened her features and framed her sweet face, which daily became peaceful and more open. It was a joy to see her transformation unfolding before my eyes.

We were all suffering from the heat which, on some days, reached almost forty-nine degrees, making activity of any kind almost impossible. I took to bucket bathing five or six times a day, and after bathing would not dry myself, but simply lie down on the cot, wet, until the hot air supped up the moisture from my skin, at which time I would bathe again.

Neil returned from Delhi and came to Shanthi with Nora to bid me farewell. We all hugged, and cried, and promised to stay in touch.

I visited the Sadhu one last time, and we renewed our plan to meet again when I returned, and to discuss my fledgling plan.

I spoke with old Brother Peter, as he chopped the vegetables alone at the table outside the dining hall. I told him I was leaving, and his eyes opened wide.

Will you return to us, Manee, he asked?

Yes, I said, I will return.

It is good, he said, for *there is a tide in the affairs of men Manee, which, if taken at the flood, leads on to adventure; omitted, the entire voyage of our lives is bound in shallows and in miseries. It is upon such a full tide that you are now afloat Manee, and you must take the current when it serves, or forever lose all of your exciting adventures*!

These adventures, my dear Manee, he said, are so much better than all the fortunes in the world!

God bless you, my lovely Brother Peter, I said, as I held his frail old body in my arms, God bless you.

Brother Joseph came out to wish me a good journey, and to invite me back to the ashram.

As I walked towards the taxi, I called back to him,

My first step away from here, Brother, is also the first step of my journey back to you.

***

Printed in Great Britain
by Amazon